If I TAKE *the* WINGS *of the* MORNING

A Cuban immigrant family's search for freedom and the challenges they faced.

DR. FELIX L. FERNANDEZ

authorHOUSE

AuthorHouse™
1663 Liberty Drive
Bloomington, IN 47403
www.authorhouse.com
Phone: 833-262-8899

This is a work of fiction. All of the characters, names, incidents, organizations, and dialogue in this novel are either the products of the author's imagination or are used fictitiously.

Published by AuthorHouse 10/15/2021

ISBN: 978-1-6655-4005-6 (sc)
ISBN: 978-1-6655-4026-1 (e)

Library of Congress Control Number: 2021920360

Print information available on the last page.

Any people depicted in stock imagery provided by Getty Images are models,and such images are being used for illustrative purposes only. Certain stock imagery © Getty Images.

This book is printed on acid-free paper.

To Ciso and Milva,

We are truly grateful you found your elusive freedom.

CHAPTER 1

In the Smokies, January 2020

Yes! Finally, success. Trying to light a fire with flint is for freaks! Nothing wrong with a match and a little lighter fluid, right? thought Quintin. As the flames grew slowly, the darkness receded, and the warmth of the fire was kind and comforting. *I can't believe those die-hard survival enthusiasts can light a bunch of twigs with a couple of rocks. Phooey! Then again, our ancestors did it routinely for thousands of years. Wow, something we take for granted, yet to them, it was vital. On the other hand, I did see my fifteen-year-old nephew do it. Ugh! In an apocalypse, I'm going to either freeze or starve to death.*

As the fire slowly grew, Quintin took a deep breath and gently blew to nurture its presence. "What is it about looking into those perpetually moving fingers of flame that stokes so many emotions, depending on one's encounter with them?" he asked aloud.

Surprisingly cool and pleasant for January, the night settled all around with an accompanying silence. As he looked around, he noted there was no wind that night to fill the pines and move their needles in sweet music. He did not even hear the sound of a cricket or the chirp of a straggling bird to accompany the background as if in a concert. Everything was still and quiet. That was all Quintin needed to put aside the past weeks' work demands.

"This is great! Love it. Yes indeed!"

Camping in the Appalachian hills of East Tennessee was a delight. Quintin, a keen admirer of history and biology, looked around at the surrounding woods and studied the trees' trunks, branches, and leaves. Even during winter and the dormancy of the season, Quintin couldn't help but feel their presence as all the different varieties of plants seemed to grow out of an entanglement of chaos. Yet he understood there was order, and life abounded for great and small alike. He inhaled deeply and took in the surrounding scent. *Such a contrast to urban living*, he thought as his memory banks chimed in.

As he sat warming by the fire, Quintin's thoughts wandered to the original inhabitants of that area, which De Soto had described in the sixteenth century. The Spanish explorer and his party had come ashore somewhere near Tampa, Florida, and slowly made their way to those ancient hills. They were credited as the first Europeans to discover the river now named the Mississippi. However, their lust for gold and riches had been matched by their cruelty.

The native inhabitants of the region must've been curious yet cautious at the appearance of the strange visitors. Wow, what an encounter that must have been.

Two worlds colliding, and eventually, one would give way. We know some of the history of when East met West through biographers and historians. However, the writers were mostly one-sided since they were the ones who told the story. Who were these indigent peoples? How did they get here? Quintin wondered. *We know relatively little of those native inhabitants. How would they view the world today? Would they even recognize their homeland? I think I was born in the wrong century. I would have loved to be present when these cultures met.*

What an adventure it must've been! he thought. *Those brave Europeans risked all they had and knew. Their own countries were becoming overcrowded and expensive, and persecution was growing. Many former soldiers serving the crown in distant lands as well as others turned their hopes and dreams to the West Indies in search of fortune and opportunity. They risked life and limb when they crossed the ocean on wooden vessels. Crazy nut jobs or courageous? Were they so desperate, or was it mostly greed?*

The Europeans' way of life had changed forever after the discovery of the Americas, but it had come at a terrible price. Once they'd discovered riches, especially gold, in the new land, an insatiable greed had been born. Native peoples would never recover from the onslaught that had befallen them over the next few centuries.

Quintin was always daydreaming of faraway places

and would imagine himself in those eras long ago. He thought of those times and the impact people's ancestors had had on the world around him, as evident in the present day. Momentous changes in history were often brutal, with no quarter given.

Us versus them, strong versus weak, rich versus poor. It was a cruel world then. Good grief, not much has really changed, he thought. *Mankind is rotten to the core, with occasional flashes of wonder and beauty. Although the surroundings were different then, are we any different? In any case, to judge our ancestors is folly. Perhaps in four hundred years, our descendants may judge us just as critically. As we look back through history, have we learned anything today? Surely the technical tools of science, medicine, communication, and transportation have improved greatly. What about the heart, our humanity, and how we view ourselves and each other? Does the heart of man truly change, or are we predictable and repetitive in our foolishness? Are the technical advances and tools we've discovered along the way helping or hurting us when we try to answer these questions?*

Quintin studied the surrounding foliage. It was thick with trees but not like the virgin forest that must've originally been there. The unspoiled, wild, and majestic oaks, hemlocks, spruces, firs, and maples that once had been there probably could have fit a small car in their trunks. *They must've been so beautiful. Some of the large rock formations and nearby boulders were probably brought here by the last ice age*, he thought, as they peeked out of the green and now mostly winter-brown surroundings.

His gaze fixed on a nearby stone the size of his cherished Jeep Wrangler. "The ages have come and gone through storms and countless nights, yet this sentinel has stood and weathered it all. If rocks could speak, what a tale they would tell," he said aloud as he smiled casually at the large boulder near him. "Good grief, I'm talking to rocks. What is wrong with me?" He looked around, hoping other campers nearby had not noticed his odd conversation with a rock. "Oh well. It's all good," he said.

Quintin loved reading any available history before visiting such places. The original inhabitants had left virtually no written record of their way of life. *Their hard lives must have been a delicate balance between everyday life and the dangers they encountered, such as weather, starvation, and unfriendly neighbors. Yet*, he wondered, *who had a better life? Perhaps they didn't live as so many of us do today, with a frenzy of stress, severe anxiety, depression, arrogance, greed, and self-centeredness. Yet they too were not strangers to danger, such as starvation, natural disasters, accidents, illness, and threats from others on the other side of the world.* Quintin's mind raced with thoughts about how they had worshipped, traded, socially interacted, fought, loved, and died. *Also, what about their migrations? Movement, yes. Did they move regularly like other cultures?*

"No doubt they had their challenges. Yet here we are in this time and this place. Who will be here next week, next year, and next century? Will mankind even be here at all? One thing is for sure: time is ruthless, unforgiving, and impartial. We are all trapped and at the mercy of time's constant march, and there are no redos," he said aloud.

Moments later, he added another log onto the fire as he settled into the chair. His wife joined him after she had finished accommodating their *mobile apartment*, a silly yet applicable term for their recreational vehicle.

"Are you in deep thought again?" she asked. "Do you have room for me wherever you're off to?"

"Hi, sweetie. You always ask me that. It's not the same without you. Sit down, and join me."

As she settled into the chair next to him, a sense of calm dominated the moment. "It's nice to go camping again and get away," she said. "We don't do this enough."

Quintin stared at the fire as if in an ancient trance.

"Evenin'," said a voice in the early evening air.

"Hello there," Quintin responded as he stood and turned to get a closer look at their visitor.

"Got me wife cookin' dinner, when she got madder than a wet hen," their camping neighbor said. The neighbor went on to explain he was staying just down the trail, in the next camping space. "Was walkin' me dog, when I thought I heard someone talkin' over here. Didn't see no other feller but you."

"Yes, well, um …" Quintin looked toward the ground and scratched the back of his head, hoping the neighbor would change the subject. His neighbor was wearing an old ball cap, a plaid shirt, and dark blue jeans and had an unkept gray beard. He was hospitable and friendly, yet Quintin thought his new friend needed an urgent bath.

"Really?" Quintin said finally. "Not a good place to be with the wife. Say, would you like some coffee?" he asked carefully, still trying to picture a mad, wet hen.

"Don't care for none. Say, young feller, that fire's no bigger than a minnow in a fishing pond. Gotta put some more logs on."

"Yes, sir. My name is Quintin," he said, and he turned to introduce his wife only to find that she was gone. *Probably went back into the camper,* he thought.

As he started to converse with his neighbor, Quintin was interrupted by a loud, unintelligible voice coming from his neighbor's camp. "Don't mind her," his neighbor said. "That's the wife. Supper must be on. Name's Buckner. Say, you're not from round here, are ya?"

"Well, no, not originally." Quintin had to concentrate in order to understand his neighbor's speech. Buckner spoke in the usual southern Appalachian dialect but seemed to speak with his mouth almost closed, and his words sounded like mumbles. "Do you guys live here in East Tennessee?" Quintin asked.

"Live over yonder." Buckner pointed toward the northeast, and Quintin was clueless as to where that could have been. "Grenvo. Been der all me life."

"Grenvo?" asked Quintin.

"Yep, Grenvo."

Then it dawned on Quintin: *He must mean Greeneville.* That was the only town he could think of that sounded remotely like what his camping neighbor described. "We live there too," said Quintin. "We've been there a couple of years. Still trying to fit in."

"Heavens to Betsy. Ya don' say," responded Buckner, smiling widely, displaying most of his missing front teeth. "Well, reckon gotta head on back. Wife gots beans and pulled pork on da fire by now. Mmm good!" He turned and walked down the trail. "Appreciate ya," he added without turning around.

Quintin watched him leave, noting a mild swagger and left lean to his walk. *Interesting character. Well, he's the current native representative of these hills,* he thought.

Moments later, Quintin returned his gaze to the small but comforting flames of the fire. His thoughts turned from local history to his early personal memories. He pondered how much his father would have loved it there. He recalled many stories his father had shared about his own youth spent growing up on a farm in western Cuba. He often had spoken of the "country way of life," the simplicity, and his love of nature and its surroundings. Quintin's thoughts turned to his father and his beloved mother, Milva.

CHAPTER 2

Daddy Day Care, 2018–2019

"How's the old man?"

"Doing great," responded Quintin's sister, Margret. "Doesn't he look good for eighty-four?"

"Frankly, no, he reminds me of where we are all heading and no one wants to go," Quintin responded.

He'd asked the question while already knowing the answer. Their father's health was deteriorating. Now, in the summer of 2019, Quintin was once again visiting his father at his group home. His sister, eternally optimistic or idealistically naive, depending on one's point of view, always seemed to have a positive spin, no matter the subject. Someone could have been passing a kidney stone the size of the Hope Diamond, and Margret would have said, "It'll pass! Don't let it get you down!" He admired his older sister, who was wickedly smart and willing to go to bat for loved ones but ruthless if she'd had enough of someone's nonsense.

Two years prior, Ciso, their father, had been subject to the Baker Act, a Florida law that allowed those in authority to have someone apprehended if they thought the person was a threat to him- or herself or someone else. Ciso had grabbed his wife, Milva, by the neck and dragged her off her hospital bed. "*Levantate*! Get up!" he'd demanded. Milva, incapacitated both mentally and physically due to a stroke, had been completely at his mercy. Ciso, still physically strong, had pulled her off the bed, dragged her across the living room, and sat her on the couch.

"Stop! Stop!" Martha, their live-in aide, had cried out.

"Shut up. My wife needs to get up. You don't know what's going on, and you don't tell me what to do!" Ciso had responded, waving his right index finger in the air.

Martha had been concerned for quite some time about the unpredictable nature of his worsening dementia and could take it no more. She'd called the police, and moments later, Ciso had been off to mental health services for evaluation and treatment, in the backseat of a police cruiser.

Milva had spent most hours of the day in a state of somnolence, with little hope of improvement, since her midbrain stroke twelve months before Ciso's detainment under the Baker Act. Although poorly equipped without any training, Ciso had insisted on personally caring for her in his home.

"No, Dad, you cannot be inserting or removing Foley catheters in your wife," Margret had argued.

Their father's worsening behavior continually tested their family's fortitude and forbearance. Quintin and his sister regularly clashed with their father as to the course of

12

treatment for their mother. They knew their father's health and memory were waning, which made things worse. He had always been a stubborn man and was used to getting things his way.

Time after time, his children argued with him on almost all aspects regarding their mother's care, including nursing care, medications, food and fluid intake, and more. Then there was the almighty financial aspect. Quintin suspected his father's insistence on keeping Milva at home served mostly as a financial gain. Ciso was in charge of the retirement pension for their mother, a retired teacher, and he would not share or allow his two children any involvement in the management of her care. Quintin had seen this before with other families who dealt with dementia. Leaving all the decisions to their ailing father was not going to end well.

Whenever Margret or Quintin approached him about helping with their mother's care, Ciso dug in, resisted, and became angrily irrational.

"There is no way I'm going to let him treat her like a sack of rice. If it was up to him, she'd be lying on an old twin mattress in the middle of the living room of their house while he tries to insert and, even worse, remove urine catheters and hand-feed and bathe her himself!" Quintin exclaimed to Margret one day. Besides, he thought, while all the arguments continued to rage, nobody thought of his mother's final wishes. The last place she would have wanted to spend the time she had left was exactly where she'd ended up: on the floor of the living room in their farmhouse. Milva never had liked living in the country and had reluctantly agreed to retire with her husband in rural South Florida, near Homestead, upon her retirement from teaching in 2004. Their home was small, but more upsetting to her was the lack of usable space, especially the tiny closets and small master bath and bedroom, not to mention the distance from her children and grandchildren. To make matters worse, she had no say in the design or layout of their so-called dream home.

Countless arguments had ensued, but Ciso refused anyone's input, especially his wife's, on their home's layout and plans. Quintin recalled several exasperated outcries from his mother, yet her husband would have none of it.

"You wouldn't be able to build this house if it wasn't for the financial contribution from my pension!" Milva would say. "*Descarado*! I should leave you, take everything, and maybe let you live in a hut for being such a prideful, stubborn ass."

"*Vete*! Leave! I don't need you or anyone" was Ciso's usual and predictable response.

Quintin would stay out of his parents' quarrels, even though in his heart, he was in agreement with his mother. Despite her threats, Ciso always seemed to get his way.

Eventually, Quintin concluded there was more to his

father's supposedly caring attitude than Ciso was willing to divulge. "Maybe I'm wrong, but I believe Dad is using our mother as a cash cow!" he told Margret.

There was no dispute from his sister. They had pleaded with their father to listen to reason regarding many aspects of her care. Ciso held all the legal cards, and even with attorney advice, there was not a lot Margret and Quintin could do.

"He listens to you more than he listens to me," Quintin told his sister.

"Well, he doesn't hear me out either," she responded.

One month prior to Ciso's Baker Act detainment in the summer of 2016, Quintin came to visit his parents at the farm. Milva had spent the last eighteen months in their living room, under hospice care. During the visit that weekend, three women came to visit with his father. They all introduced themselves to Quintin politely, yet Quintin thought the meeting seemed out of place. The women were not related to each other, and neither he nor his sister, Margret, knew anything about them. One woman seemed fit; was dressed in a T-shirt, blue jeans, and boots; and went by the name of Estela. Standing next to her, Odalys introduced herself. She spoke only Spanish and had a daughter just out of her teenage years called Ana. Lastly, Tina was petite, had dirty-blonde hair, and rarely smiled. She did most of the talking in a heavy Spanish accent, and it seemed to Quintin the other two took her lead.

Each of them had arrived from Cuba less than two years prior. As the details of their visit slowly became apparent, Quintin realized they were arranging to live on-site at the farm. It had been agreed that Estela would work the small farm, and Odalys would see to Milva's needs. Apparently, the current caregiver, Martha, who had been taking care of Milva for the past six months, was going to receive walking papers. Tina would fill in whatever role was necessary. Odalys's daughter, Ana, would bring a trailer to live with her boyfriend next to the small guesthouse behind the main residence. It was apparent she and her boyfriend would live on the property for free. Quintin saw the potential abuse, and it made his skin crawl.

With small talk out of the way, Quintin was increasingly uneasy with their proposed arrangement and sensed ulterior motives.

As two of the women went into the house to converse with Ciso, Quintin spoke with Estela regarding yard and animal care. Estela confided that she was concerned about Ciso. One week earlier, she had met with Ciso on the farm to go over details regarding farm upkeep and maintenance, when, she informed Quintin, an unusual incident had occurred. While she and Ciso had been walking in the mango grove, he'd started explaining fertilizer and water needs for the plants. According to her, Ciso had made little sense and seemed to mumble incoherently. During their walk, he'd spotted what he thought was a man hiding behind one of the mango trees. He immediately had stopped what he was saying and had run to the shed, come out with a long machete, and chased the supposed stranger.

Estela said, "He yelled, '*Te voy a matar*! *Te voy a matar*!' He kept yelling while he chased the trespasser."

"Who was on the property?" Quintin asked.

"That's just it. There was no one there. I thought he had lost his mind and would come after me, so I ran to my car and left as soon as possible. He called me several hours later, and after I informed him of what I had seen, he apologized. Does your father drink?"

"Socially but not enough that would explain something like that," he responded. Quintin's mind raced. His father not only was having memory lapses but also was hallucinating. *Ay Dios*, he thought.

Moments later, Tina came over and started to discuss living arrangements. According to her, they would not pay any rent, only partial utility bills, per an agreement between them and Ciso. For Quintin, having five strange adults living on the property rent free with no contract and trusting they would care for his ailing mother and elderly father, who was obviously experiencing hallucinations, was more than he could bear. "That will not be acceptable," he said.

"Well, our arrangement is not with you but with your father," Tina snapped.

Quintin looked for his father and saw him speaking to young Ana near the dining room. He had a stupid grin on his face like a pathetic, lovestruck puppy. Quintin was concerned for his parents, fearing that these individuals were going to take advantage of the situation. "Like I said, this is not going to happen. There needs to be a contract, and you will deal with me and my sister. Period. End of story!"

"Eh? *Que te pasa cabron*?" Tina raised her voice at Quintin and said a few profane words in Spanish.

Quintin had had enough. "You people have exactly two minutes to get off our property before I throw you out and have you arrested for trespassing!"

The strangers voiced a few more choice words as they slowly got back into their vehicle and left. While driving off, one of the ladies lowered her window, displayed her middle finger, and yelled, "Fuck you, man!"

Shortly thereafter, Quintin explained to his father what had just happened. Ciso became angry and told his son never to interfere with his personal business dealings again. Quintin reminded him that his mother's delicate state was in the balance and said he would not have strangers, much less someone not trained, care for her.

Ciso was adamant. "Stay out of my affairs!" he yelled.

"While my mother lives, that's not going to happen,

viejo!" Quintin walked away angrily before he acted on what was on his mind: picking his father up and throwing him against the wall.

A few minutes later, as Quintin was preparing to leave, he spoke to Martha, their current caregiver. Prior to her, there had been two previous caregivers. Ciso had fired them and was planning on dismissing Martha as well. Martha was in her mid-seventies but had many years of experience in caring for elderly families. She had been carefully vetted by Margret and came recommended by trusted sources.

"I'm leaving today," Quintin told Martha. "If I stay and listen to his crap for one more minute, I'm gonna bust!"

"Relax. I'll watch him, and I'll especially watch your mom. I'm not gonna let anything happen to her."

Quintin gave her a smile and then a hug before he walked to his car.

"*Acuerdate, el no esta bien.*" Her reminder that his father was not well allowed peace to return to Quintin's heart, and the flame of anger receded.

On the drive to his in-laws' home, Quintin prayed, but he knew he and Margret had to prepare for a coming storm.

The next several months were no picnic. Ciso continued to experience hallucinations. At first, they were short-lived and appeared nonthreatening. He was manageable at first, but slowly, things started to worsen. Margret and her husband spent many weekends driving down and staying with him while Martha did what she could.

Milva finally passed away three months later, in September 2016. When Quintin and his sister broke the news to Ciso, "*O cara*" was his only response, and then he nodded and continued feeding his chickens.

Quintin reflected on their fifty-seven-year marriage. As the memories flooded his mind, he recognized their marriage as a testament to their commitment to stay together and endure the many trials and challenges they faced. As with many couples of their time, putting up with each other's crap for so long had to speak for something. They were diametrically different, with opposing likes, dreams, and visions for themselves and their family, yet somehow, they were able to keep it together. In Quintin's and Margret's hearts, part of them wished their parents would've divorced and avoided the many heated quarrels. But somewhere deep inside him, Quintin took comfort that they hadn't. *Modern-day couples would've abandoned their relationships long before*, he thought.

The death of their mother hit harder than either one of them had expected. Everyone, especially Quintin, knew about the delicate nature of their mother's health. Standing by and waiting for his mother to pass, Quintin was emotionally ready for the news, or so he thought. Margret explained to him that their mother had had difficulty breathing, and a hospice nurse had tried to administer medication to ease her struggle. With her chronically weakened state, after only a few minutes, she had seemed to relax and then had quietly stopped breathing. The news hit Quintin hard, despite his being ready for the inevitable, given what they had been experiencing over the past eighteen months.

He informed his staff at the office and left for the day. He shared the news with his wife and two children when he arrived home. The woman he'd adored and who he knew had loved him unconditionally was gone. No anticipation, preparation, or training could have eased his grief.

Shortly after delivering the news to Quintin over the phone, Margret was overcome with her own grief and suffered a sudden onset of chest pain that landed her in the nearest emergency room. She was relieved to know what she had already suspected: they diagnosed her with a panic attack. It was a state of the heart, and she was released after a few hours.

Margret called her brother later that evening and said, "She was a better mother than I was a daughter." Her voice cracked with emotion as the weight of the loss of her mother and past memories surfaced without mercy.

As the days marched on following Milva's death, Ciso continued a stair step decline. There were moments of cognitive stability followed by steep neurological or psychological changes. The situation became difficult and heartbreaking to watch.

Quintin remembered having a short, pleasant conversation with his father one morning on their farm, when something caught Ciso's attention. As he stared out the dining room window, Ciso slowly rose from the table and gazed at the front porch of the guesthouse just fifty feet away. "*Mira, mira.* Look at the size of that dog."

Quintin's heart sank when he realized there was no such thing. He just stared at his aging father. Moments later, Quintin reached for a nearby glass of water and tried to drink. As his heart sank, such a flood of emotion rushed Quintin that he had a difficult time swallowing.

Slowly and relentlessly, with each passing week, their father was slipping into cognitive darkness. Two weeks following Milva's funeral, Martha was unable to care for him any longer. His erratic behavior and verbal outbursts were overwhelming. He needed a more stable environment, and Margret stepped right in. After searching for days, she found a small place willing and able to care for him. Ciso eventually came to reside in a skilled home with continuous care.

When he first arrived in October 2016, he was capable of basic communication with the staff. He appeared physically weak but was still able to stand. His memory-recall ability worsened with each passing week. During one of Quintin's visits to the nursing facility, he tried to engage his father. "Dad, it's me. Talk to me," he said as his sister, Margret, hand-fed their father. As she lived only forty minutes away, it was Margret who bore the brunt of his care.

The converted home, with a dozen other residents and nursing on hand, was simple yet practical. Most of the other residents were ladies, and since Ciso was the handsome new resident, several wanted to marry him or at least get his attention. Perhaps unaware of their intentions, Quintin seized on the opportunity to encourage a reaction. "Dad, Ms. Iglesias thinks you are very good looking. What do you have to say to that?"

Ciso attempted a small and short smile but was mostly unfazed. It appeared to Quintin as though his father were doing all he could just to stay in the present. He struggled to answer basic questions and couldn't hold a conversation beyond one sentence. Quintin sensed an internal struggle within his father that broke his heart, as he knew there was not much anyone could do for him.

His slow two-year decline accelerated as the summer of 2019 gave way to fall. He declined physically at first, and then he experienced worsening awareness. In the following months, he became what he often had feared: dependent on others.

It is foolish to think we have a choice as to how and when we depart this one and only life, thought Quintin.

He thought of Milva's passing three years before. It had been difficult, as it should have been to lose one's mother, but it had come as a final relief to Quintin, given her slow atrophy and ever-worsening, pitiful condition. Bedbound since her stroke, during her last few weeks, she'd declined in health without any appreciable improvement, despite hospice's valiant efforts.

Over the course of a few short months, Ciso kept losing weight, and his walking became dangerously unstable. He had verbal outbursts, followed by physical altercations with others in the group home, as his cognitive awareness continued to wane. *It's gotta be a combination of vascular and Alzheimer's dementia*, Quintin thought. Ciso would have seemingly attentive and proper moments and then suddenly have steep psychological and emotional declines. All the while, his short-term memory was rapidly eroding. It was now almost gone. In the months leading to Ciso's skilled nursing admission, he had been hallucinating, despite being treated with a cocktail of psychotropic medications by psychiatrists and neurologists. His erratic behavior, coupled with stubborn pride, made him a difficult patient for anyone to treat and stabilize, much less improve.

Still, Quintin felt a deep love for the man who had led his family to a distant shore many years before. He had risked it all for the sake of freedom for himself, his wife, and, mostly, his young children. Although Quintin felt an array of emotions, his devotion and admiration for his father ruled the day. He had to put aside the many quarrels he and his sister had had with their father over the past couple of years. He still felt a deep love for the man who had led his family through thick and thin.

The grief of their mother's passing was deep and would hit Quintin and his sister in waves, as only deep sorrow could. Milva's favorite things, such as Bee Gees music and classic movies, reminded them of her. Quintin had adored his mother, and they always had been close. "I was a true mama's boy," he often said.

Quintin had treated dementia in his practice; however, dealing with his father's condition was personal. His thoughts were often filled with memories of many patients and their families trying to cope with that horrible disease, which stole the mind and crushed loved ones in its path.

"Dad, look at me. Open your eyes. It's Quintin and Margret. We are here. *Abre los ojos!*"

Ciso would sometimes open his eyes for a brief moment but would rarely lock onto his children's faces. He would stare around the room and mumble incoherent words that sounded like names of friends or family from long ago.

"He hallucinates almost all the time now," said Margret. "I wonder who or what he sees. Sometimes he mentions people's names. Occasionally, I can recognize one or two."

"Did he mention Mom or *Abuelo* Felix?" asked Quintin.

"No, but I did pick up Lipio. He was sitting up, mumbling as he usually does, staring at the wall, and said his name. It kind of creeped me out," Margret said while adjusting Ciso's bed position to avoid pressure on his back. They both hated seeing him like that, withering away as mortality and the march of time reigned together. The once proud leader of his family and fiercely independent man was quickly slipping away.

Quintin stared at his aging father, hoping for an acknowledgment of any kind. The photo on the nightstand of his parents taken long ago caught Quintin's eye, and Margret noticed her brother staring at the photograph. "Was that picture taken before we left Cuba?" he asked.

"Yep, sometime right before leaving. Mom told me it was taken shortly after he was released from the work camp. I'm telling you, he's going to be with us for several more years. You'll see!" Margret said as she dismissed her father's obvious decline over the past few months as she looked at him.

Quintin's heart and mind were out of sync with each other. His heart ached for a miraculous awakening. His mind pushed back with inarguable reality. "Don't know about that, Sis," he said. His mind was trying hard to remember anything of the years long ago and the stories his parents had told him.

CHAPTER 3

Cuba, 1959

It was July 1959. Ciso and Lipio were waiting for Herman as they hid in a small patch of woods. Pinar del Río was the westernmost province in Cuba. Known for its rich soil, the entire area was heavily farmed. The region was well known for its excellent tobacco, which, in the 1950s, was exported all over the world.

Ciso's father, Felix, had begun his family business in the early 1920s, delivering farm goods to local bodegas or country stores off the bed of a flatbed truck. With demand growing for necessities, it wasn't long before his little growing enterprise demanded serious attention. In time, he bought the plot adjacent to his homestead, worked the land, and added vehicles and personnel to his truck fleet. Working tirelessly, the young entrepreneur was ambitious and eventually quite prosperous. With fertile soil, produce, including malanga, yucca, avocados, and corn, were regulars and in demand. Fruits, such as papayas, mangoes, and guavas, were also readily consumed and purchased at his open-air markets. He tried his hand at other commercial enterprises; however, he was less successful with many of them.

"I started at least twenty different businesses during that time. I failed at most of them but succeeded in one or two, and that was all that was needed," he later claimed.

The 1930s were difficult years everywhere, and Cuba was no exception. At twenty-six years of age, Felix met a local farmer's daughter who was working at one of his bodegas. After a two-year courtship, he and Margo were married in the summer of 1932.

"She was simple and hardworking. That was all," he said later.

Margo was also uncharacteristically tall. At five foot ten, she towered over women and most men, including Felix. It was rumored she was not allowed to wear heeled shoes. Nine months after their marriage, their first son, Alex, was born, and one year later, their second son, Ciso, came into the world. They had three children in all; the youngest was their one and only daughter.

During the late 1930s, Felix began planting acres of tobacco with newly acquired acreage while steadily expanding economically. Then, during the Second World War, Cuba's economy expanded. The Allies were in need of just about any and all consumable goods, including sugar and cigars. Felix's enterprises, which included several well-established bodegas and one of the region's only corn mills, were booming.

The 1950s brought Fulgencio Batista back into politics, as he led a coup and won in 1952. The takeover did not sit well with many Cubans, especially one: Fidel Castro. Fidel made it difficult for elections over the next several years while threatening voters with violent retribution and execution if they dared to vote in the 1958 elections. However, to most of the general population, Castro was an alternative to the current regime, which many concluded was illegitimate. Some believed Batista had trampled their constitution. During those politically turbulent years, the Fernandez family and many others found themselves having to maneuver through life however possible.

"*Donde esta* Herman?" asked Ciso as he wiped sweat off his brow in the unrelenting tropical heat and humidity of the Caribbean.

"*Tranquilo, él viene,*" said Lipio, "Just hold on, *chico!*"

Despite the thickness of the foliage, Ciso couldn't help but notice the beautiful royal poincianas scattered about, as if each tree claimed its own piece of real estate to show off its beauty. Their bright orange flowers stood out among the lush green tropical surroundings. From their elevated vantage point, he could see several farms in the distance. Ciso's thoughts momentarily drifted to his childhood days spent running through the vast farms near his home, not far from where they stood now. As he thought about those years of working on his father's farm, he remembered his family ties to that land going back several generations. He and Lipio, now in their mid-twenties, knew the area well. Presently, however, fear and uncertainty gripped him with the growing chaos they had faced during the last several years.

After Batista led his coup d'état, constitutionalists felt betrayed, and they plotted, hoping for the return of constitutionality. The politically explosive environment in Havana was spreading, and it felt toxic and repulsive to some Cubans. Many had already fled the island. Countless roundups, imprisonments, and subsequent beatings of dissenters who disagreed with Batista's government gripped the country.

"Batista *es un puerco*," Lipio said while showing his pearly whites with his usual exaggerated smile.

Ciso's thoughts were interrupted by Lipio's comment. As Ciso's gaze turned toward him, they heard what sounded like a diesel engine quickly approaching. Full of nervous anxiety, they stayed low at their predetermined rendezvous. *Was Herman followed? Did he remember where to meet? Did he bring all the cargo?* As Ciso's mind raced with questions, both men looked down the trail to see whom or what they were up against.

As the truck approached, they could see the familiarity of the light blue 1953 Chevy and let out sighs of relief. Herman had finally made it. As he approached, he slowed the vehicle while Ciso and Lipio revealed themselves to him. The three of them were relieved and a little surprised they had made it this far.

Several months earlier, they had contacted El Mejicano, a Mexican arms dealer they had met through an ex-army officer who wanted the return to a lawful constitution brought forward with the removal of Batista. After two meetings with him, the trio had rounded up the funds necessary for the purchase of weapons now in the truck.

"You made it," said Ciso.

"*Cla, cla, claro*," responded Herman.

So far, everything had gone according to plan. The men prepared to divvy up the arms. Their plan was to bury their cargo until a predetermined time.

"This is only the beginning. Soon the people will rally and overthrow *los desgraciados*," Lipio said, still smiling from ear to ear.

"Aha, *si*," responded Herman.

Moments later, an unsettling noise down the hill disrupted their jovial conversation.

"*Callate la boca*," said Ciso, cautioning the others to be quiet and listen.

Herman ran to get a better look down the trail. "No, no, no. *No puede ser*" (This cannot be), he muttered. Turning quickly to the other two, he informed them that a small armed police unit personnel carrier was headed in their direction.

"*Idiota!*" cried Ciso. "They followed you up here, and now we are all going to be arrested and probably shot."

Herman was now visibly shaking, and his stutter worsened to the point that the only words he was able to voice were "*Ay Dios*" as he rubbed the back of his head.

"It must have been one of the farmers," Lipio said.

"But they were sympathetic to our cause," responded a surprised Ciso with an angry tone. "*Coño*! How can they betray us like this? Don't they know it is for their own good? *Que hacemos*? You know what they will do if they find us with these rifles?"

The three looked at one other and knew what they had to do. With no military training, they dropped everything and ran. Ciso and Lipio took off into the woods southeast as fast as they could, while Herman headed in another direction. There was no time to think; they all ran toward their respective homes, not knowing where else to go. Fleeting thoughts of standing before a firing squad terrified Ciso. As they ran for their lives, they knew their hard work and planning could end with the weapons confiscated and possibly their identities known.

"*Co, co, corre!*" Herman yelled.

Their planning and dreams of contributing to the downfall of the Batista regime were wrecked.

It was late in the evening before Ciso made it back to his father's farm. *How can this be happening? We had the support of the locals.* Ciso's thoughts turned to the safety of his family.

After arriving home late in the evening, he spent the night watching and waiting.

The following morning, Ciso came out of the cigar barn, where he had spent the night. As he approached the rear of the house, near the kitchen, he saw one of the young housemaids leaving, looking down as she buttoned her blouse. He could see his father, Felix, near the kitchen table, unaware that his son had seen him and was aware of his philandering. The family had suspected, and now Ciso was convinced, his father was sleeping with the hired help.

Ciso approached him, and as he was mustering the courage to question his father, Felix abruptly asked his son where he had been all night.

"*Con mis amigos,*" he replied.

"*Cambiate la ropa. Hay que trabajar!*" barked his father.

Having more pressing things on his mind, Ciso changed his clothes and went to work with his father, as he had for most of his life. The fear of Batista's federal troops arriving at any moment to arrest him and jeopardize his family was a terrifying thought he could not bear. In addition, if Felix found out what he and the other two rebels were up to, retribution would be swift and unpleasant. Ciso eyed his father a few feet away. As he worked the farm that day, it became clear to him: he had to leave the country.

CHAPTER 4

Poopies, Summer 1986

"Don't eyeball me, boy! Keep your eyes straight, you maggot! You ain't got no discipline, boy. In fact, all you girls are taking up oxygen. You don't deserve to become naval aviators. Fifty! Get 'em!" yelled the gunnery sergeant.

The commonly used command implied dropping to the floor in a push-up position and commencing with fifty push-ups without stopping and with the possibility of more being added, depending on the drill instructor's current mood. Bending the waist or back or touching the ground with one's knees was never tolerated. Each push-up was verbally counted when done, and if there was any infraction, the count started again from the beginning.

Only sixty seconds earlier, Quintin and the other aviation officer candidates had awakened to the mind-numbing noise of aluminum trash cans being thrown onto the concrete floor, along with screaming and yelling from United States Marine Corps drill instructors. The instructors' sole purpose was to see if the new candidates—or poopies, as they were called—had what it took to earn an officer commission and, eventually, wings of gold to become United States naval aviators.

While one of the gunnery sergeants poked the edge of his Smokey Bear hat into Quintin's forehead, the other drill instructors (DIs) were yelling at the other candidates in what appeared to be a coordinated—and successful—attempt at absolute yet synchronized chaos. This was the pressure cooker: fourteen weeks of gut-wrenching physical, emotional, and psychological pressure designed to tear them down, see what they were made of, and, if they survived, build them back up again the navy way.

As they were ordered to muster in front of the building, some of the new poopies tripped over others doing push-ups in their rush to get outside.

"Hey, Sarge!" yelled one of the staff sergeants. "Come take a look at this boy's head! It looks as though he has mange."

"What? Mange? My dog has mange!" said one of the other DIs.

"Don't touch it; it might be contagious," said Staff Sergeant Jones.

By then, several drill instructors were staring at the singled-out candidate's shaved head while he was on his face. They followed their jeering with more comments and chuckles.

"On your feet, girls!" barked the gunnery sergeant.

The entire class was then ordered to line up in front of the regimental building. The candidates were arranged four across shoulder to shoulder and thirteen deep. Most of them had only seen military formation on television or in the movies, and the ensuing attempt was expectedly chaotic. The poopies were already profusely sweating at 0530, disorganized and confused.

"You bunch of morons!" the gunny yelled.

Just when Quintin thought they were getting in step, two drill instructors took turns screaming into his ear and then moved on to the next candidate. They began endless drills, which included instructions on formation marching, turns, about-faces, saluting, proper duties of a sentry, and how to wear a uniform properly, among many other repetitive drills.

The to-memorize list was long, and each candidate was expected to master all of it perfectly. When evening finally came, an exhausted Quintin stared at the ceiling while in his bunk, pondering the day's experience. During the evening hours, the poopies were allowed downtime. That included time to study the day's information and the academics of any course or classroom material covered that day. Quintin felt the day's intense experiences still permeating through him. Physically exhausted, he felt as if his nervous system had been jolted by a bolt of lightning, and his mind was still in hyperdrive. *I don't know if I'm gonna make it through this*, he thought. As he took a moment after organizing his personal belongings, he was able to observe his three roommates. He felt relieved to see that they looked just as pitiful as he did.

"Well, that was day one. Thirteen weeks and six days to go," said one of his roommates. Quintin recognized him as the poor soul the drill instructors had been laughing at with mange. "I'm Scottie," he said.

Small talk ensued between the four bunkmates after they introduced themselves. They had been together for the last sixteen hours yet knew nothing about each other. Quintin and his roommates were relieved to learn it was not mange but a rather large birthmark on Scottie's scalp. Scottie, from Boston, was the son and grandson of army majors. Quintin initially thought he was from New York because of his accent. *Boston, New York—same crap*, Quintin thought.

Jim, the tallest of the four, was from Arkansas. He had a predictable southern draw and smiled often, proudly showing off his large yellow teeth. Quintin thought, *I hope he's not a redneck.* He then asked, "Hey, Jim, do you guys have any Cubans in Arkansas?"

Jim paused for a moment and then responded, "Only the ones hanging from trees." Quintin's three roommates roared with laughter. After a slight delay, Quintin did as well.

Every morning, with a single command from the drill instructor, they ran in formation for a crisp three-mile jog just after five o'clock. Only three days earlier, they had all reported as civilians to the regiment after passing an extensive physical exam. Now, as a cohesive group, they were assigned to class 38-86, the thirty-eighth class for 1986. With their heads shaved, stripped of identities and reduced to the level of something resembling irrelevant bacteria, they carried on. The grueling daily schedule remained pretty much the same.

As was customary, later that evening, the senior candidate officers were available to answer questions and help the new guys get adjusted to their new home. Quintin and the rest of his classmates found them to be helpful, and the senior classmates gave each of them fresh insight. Their presence helped the new class gain perspective on all aspects of life in AOCS, including marching, how to wear a uniform, proper saluting, spit-shining boots, general procedures, and what to expect over the weeks ahead. Each week seemed to bring on new challenges they all had to absorb. Every time the candidate officers spoke, they had everyone's undivided attention. These were upperclassmen getting ready to graduate the following week.

Quintin returned to his room after a welcome shower down the hall. He was wrapped in his standard-issue white towel and wore rubber sandals with his name stamped on them. All personal belongings were stamped with names, especially clothes. Laundry was handled in bulk all at once. The last thing they all wanted was to wear someone else's skivvies, especially the females in the class.

"Good evening, Candidate. I'm Candidate Officer Jack Jones."

Quintin stood at attention as the soon-to-be commissioned officer entered the room.

"Where are your roommates?" he asked.

"Sir, the candidates are in the head, showering," responded a startled Quintin.

"This bed is a disaster. Clean it, and dress it."

"Yes, s—"

Quintin was promptly cut off before he could answer. The upperclassman continued to list off a litany of inadequacies that needed to be addressed. "You are a disgrace, Candidate. You can't do anything right, you spic!"

Quintin's eyes momentarily locked onto the upperclassman and then quickly stared forward. He was not sure what to say or how to answer. The candidate officer glared back at him and then promptly exited the room.

Quintin only had a brief moment to digest what had just transpired before one of his roommates came in, still wet from his shower. Quintin went to sleep that night wondering about the exchange he'd had with the upperclassman. *Dirtbag. Racist piece of turd. I'm not gonna let him or any other asshole stop me from flying fighters. Whatever!* he thought. Less than a minute later, completely exhausted, he saw the back of his eyelids.

The new candidates had a long way to go before becoming the officers the navy intended them to be. Two weeks into indoctrination into Aviation Officer Candidate School, Quintin kept wondering, *What the hell did I get myself into? I wanted to fly jets.* That seemed far off and still very much a dream right then. Each day began at 0500 and ended at 1900, followed by two hours of study time before the playing of taps and lights-out promptly at 2200. The physical demands were designed to take the young candidates to the brink of collapse to determine how well they were able to recover, their overall attitude, and how much stamina they had. Most challenging for Quintin were the psychological challenges. No matter how well a task was accomplished, it never seemed to be good enough, and that fact was broadcast to all. Even breathing was a privilege that did not seem good enough. The candidates were constantly reminded the only privilege granted to them was the choice to DOR (drop on request). Meals, rest, and relieving oneself were not considered privileges.

After returning from the three-mile run, class 38-86 marched into the chow hall—the cafeteria—for their first meal of the day. *Ah*, thought Quintin, *finally something to eat and drink and a chance to sit down.*

"Keep your eyes on your trays, maggots! Do not eyeball the area!" shouted one of the drill instructors on one of the first days.

The candidates made their way back to their tables and stood behind their chairs, waiting for the signal to sit and eat. Quintin and his classmates were like pets in training, waiting for the signal from the master. His belly growled; he couldn't wait to scarf down his meal, whatever it was. He dared not glance at the surrounding room and his neighbors. However, with his curiosity burning, he took a split-second glance at the other table.

Moments later, he felt tugging on his neck, and he realized that the fingers of the drill instructor were grabbing his dog tag chain and yanking him out of lineup just before they were about to receive the order to sit and eat. Like a dog on a leash, he was held tightly, barely able to move. "You eyeballed the area, scum bucket!"

How can this be? Quintin thought. *I only glanced for a split second.* Unfortunately, that was all that was needed to break the uniformity of the group and get the gunnery sergeant's attention.

"You have exactly fifteen seconds to eat your grub while standing."

"Sir, yes, sir" was the only accepted response at any time from any candidate.

"Fifty, boy. Get 'em."

With his meal half eaten and just about reaching his stomach, he pumped out the dreaded push-ups, about to revisit what he had just consumed. *I should've listened to my old man and not joined this man's navy*, thought Quintin as he continued his push-ups over his once-eaten breakfast now on the floor beneath him.

CHAPTER 5

Revolución, 1960

Upon returning to his country after being gone for almost a full year, Ciso couldn't help but notice the thick political atmosphere that had developed. As some had expected, immediately following the Cuban revolution, an unsettling presence gripped the country, and just about everyone had an opinion. However, Ciso observed that not all were willing to voice their opinions openly.

"How are things going?" he would casually ask while standing in line for *cafecito* and pastries.

"Bien," some responded. Most, however, would look around and not answer or would politely walk away.

He had heard of the secret police cracking down on dissent. He refused to believe it. *Bunch of paranoid freaks*, he thought. For now, Ciso's thoughts were increasingly about his friends Herman and Lipio, who had run with him from Batista's local militia almost a year prior. Had they been captured, imprisoned, beaten, or, worse, executed? Leaving Havana's airport, he noticed uniformed soldiers everywhere. Castro had just seized power, and some of his supporters filled the streets. Those civilians seemed intolerant of others' opinions, as Ciso watched several middle-aged men get grabbed, beaten, and taken away by those in uniform. *I must get out of the city,* he thought. He managed to procure transportation as he attempted to make his way back to his father's farm.

As he approached the province of Pinar del Río two hours later, the royal palms, rich soil, and farm fields were familiar and welcoming. He felt a flood of emotions, followed by a clear-cut cognizance of fear. Had he and his companions been identified? Would it matter to the new regime? *It must be to our benefit. The new regime must see us as useful to their cause,* he thought, since he and his two comrades had attempted to aid the fall of the Batista regime one year earlier.

He thought of his parents, brother, and younger sister. He'd had minimal correspondence with them while he was in Europe and even less with his fiancée, Milva. His brother, Ramon, had found favor with the Castro regime, which, although now in power, had not yet solidified their grip on the country. Pockets of pro-Batista and anti-Castro elements were being dealt with. Ciso partially kept in touch with his family thanks to his father, who'd helped to financially support him while he was in Europe.

Now that Batista was gone, Ciso felt it was reasonably safe to finally come home. He had heard disturbing reports of recent assassinations and property seizures. The press was restricted, and commerce was grinding to a halt. *It's all temporary,* he thought. *We need a Cuba rooted in laws. Besides, things can't get any worse after that criminal*

Batista abused our constitution, he told himself. *The newly established government just needs time to adjust.*

The central highway was still relatively clear as the bus slowly made its way west. *I can't wait to get home.* While away, he'd had a lot of time to think about what he wanted his life to look like going forward in the current situation. Few things mattered more to him than family. Torn by the love he had for them and the idealism of youth, he seldom had peace, at least not yet. As he looked around at the faces of his countrymen, he sensed an uncomfortable tension. Initially, he tried to dismiss it as a consequence of the momentous changes taking place on the island. However, with so many awkward changes, he also felt uneasy. Ciso's mind and heart felt as if they were on distant shores with a vast ocean between them. *Freedom, you are so elusive. Why do you have to be so?* he thought.

When he returned from Western Europe, the reminders of a long, brutal fight for their survival during the First and Second World Wars were still fresh and unmistakable. Their freedoms would be preserved from the onslaught of Nazi and Fascist totalitarianism. However, Eastern Europe woke to a different fate at the end of World War II. The Soviet Union now had an iron grip and was well entrenched throughout the eastern countries in Europe. Europe was one continent with two opposing political realities with clear differences. In addition, Marxist ideology was spreading worldwide.

Ciso thought long and hard about Europe's current standing and Cuba's destiny. *We all just need to do our part and continue to follow the breadcrumbs to liberty one day at a time*, he concluded.

O cara, sometimes I wish I could fly to a faraway place. Perhaps there I could find her, that elusive peace that only freedom can bring, he thought as the aging bus stopped and picked up an elderly couple. *God, did we do the right thing?* he wondered. Batista had fled, and a new governance and direction were taking shape. As events on the island continued to slowly unfold, to Ciso, the clear path forward he'd believed in one year ago was no longer evident. His heart grew ever more troubled. Slowly, though he didn't realize it at the time, he was running out of bread crumbs.

Ciso's father, Felix, was the cornerstone of the family with his strong will and business savvy. He had built wealth through local trucking deliveries and tobacco. Ciso's mother, Margo, had always been there for him and his siblings, only to be plagued in her fifties with Parkinson's and its debilitating outcome. In addition, her troubled marriage made her health situation worse. Ciso's brother had started law school in Havana one year before the revolution, only to have those dreams dashed with the start of the revolution. The brothers looked after their sister Rita, who'd been named after a deceased aunt, since she was younger, and to them, she was the prettiest girl in town. She was ten years younger than Ciso, the result of his parents' reconciliation after a tempestuous split seventeen years earlier. He always tried to look after her, and recently, thoughts about her boyfriend plagued him.

"He's not a hard worker. In fact, he's a lazy ass," he told Rita and his brother Alex. "Sooner or later, he is going to be a burden to you and our family." He didn't want that *come mierda* around.

Rita would have none of it. "*Yo lo quiero!*" she would often cry, and the resulting drama was enough to end the discussion.

Their father, Felix, was not on board with their expectant engagement, yet he too did nothing to discourage, much less prevent, the relationship. She was Daddy's girl.

"Spoiled brat. I hope she wakes the hell up," Alex said.

Once they were out of Havana Province and entering familiar territory, Ciso's thoughts were interrupted by the screeching of the old bus's brakes. All traffic was forced to stop at a roadblock ahead. Several men in green military fatigues were conducting searches of vehicles on the road. Everyone on the bus was told to disembark, and each passenger was questioned.

One of the uniformed men, with a thick black mustache and beard, came to Ciso and asked, "Who are you? Show us your identification." But before he could answer the first question, he was asked a second.

Ciso's apprehension turned to anger. *He has the manners of a pig*, he thought.

After a brief moment, Ciso was cleared. As he watched the officers interact with the passengers, one of the uniformed men seemed particularly interested in a passenger sitting toward the back of the bus. After a short exchange of words, one of the officers asked for his name.

"Nicolas," the passenger responded while presenting identification, when the two uniformed men suddenly grabbed him by both arms, forced him off the bus, and placed him in the back of one of their cars.

"*Alludenme, por favor!*" yelled the man as two men shoved him. The officers yelled for him to shut up, even after he presented his government identification.

To Ciso, the episode seemed out of place. *That man had to have done something horribly wrong to be taken away like that*, he thought.

One of the passengers tried to help the poor man only to be slapped and pushed away. She was left shaking, holding the right side of her stricken face. Seconds later, the officers closed the door of their vehicle and quickly drove off. Ciso and the other passengers, afraid they too would be accosted, looked on, horrified, but kept their mouths shut. The checkpoint guard told them to reboard the bus and then cleared them on their way.

The passengers resumed their trip, too stunned to say anything. Ciso thought about the poor bastard they'd arrested and wondered what terrible crime he had been accused of and what his fate would be. The man had seemed to do everything right, answering their questions and presenting appropriate documents, yet they still had taken him without any charges. *Very strange*, he thought.

As he looked at the faces of the passengers, he was struck by their blank stares, which seemed to hide something worse. Uncertainty perhaps. But fear was present and on full display. *Que esta pasando?* he thought. *What the hell was that all about? Something doesn't seem right. Can't think about that right now. I just want to get home. Besides, I know eventually things will improve. It's still too early. Yes, too early for any normalcy*, he told himself.

Several hours after his trip began, Ciso exited the bus on the main road. He had a short walk to his home. He welcomed the sight of mangoes, avocados, and guavas ripening in the hot July sun. Many of the nearby fields were oddly unplanted, and there was no one in sight. *Strange. Must be the heat*, he thought.

When he arrived home, relief encompassed him as he saw that his family were indeed safe. He was also glad to hear that both of his rebellious companions were alive and well. Herman had fled to Mexico and was still there, aided by his father, who had substantial financial means. Lipio had hidden for several months in a small village on the southern coast known for its fishing. Now that the Batista government had been disbanded and no one had come looking for him, Lipio felt safe and recently had come out of hiding. He was helping Felix on the farm.

After a couple of days at home, Ciso made a special trip to see his fiancée, Milva, at her house. She lived with her parents, Luis and Micaela; her aging aunt Liche; and her special-needs younger brother, Oswald, in a two-bedroom home along the main street in San Juan y Martínez. Her older brother, Luis Jr., had finished his medical studies at the university one year earlier. The small country town where she lived was a conventional Cuban town with simplicity and old-world charm. As in many small towns, everyone knew one other and knew almost everything about one another. The most popular and exciting venue was the local theater, where they played Hollywood's most current films. Milva loved films. *Gone with the Wind* was her favorite. "Clark Gable is so handsome," she often said. "I would marry him tomorrow, even if he is much older." Her older brother had recently moved back and opened his medical practice in town so he could be close to family and help whenever they needed it.

Milva was glad to see Ciso, and they embraced cautiously under her mother's watchful eye. Her father, Luis, owned the dance hall next to their home. It had been the scene of many weddings and festive occasions during the 1940s and 1950s. Now, however, the building sat vacant and unused. It was as if its former glory had passed with all the political changes that had occurred. Luis was a quiet man and kept mostly to himself more and more. Family and friends had noticed the not-so-subtle change in him, and Milva was becoming concerned. His career as a professional baseball player in the 1920s had been cut short due to a devastating ankle injury. He'd put his efforts into the business of running the dance hall, where he and his wife, Micaela, had provided an escape for many in their little town. It had been a place for dancing, singing, and having conversations about the latest and greatest current events, including politics. Whatever the topic, it had been openly discussed.

Cubans tended to be passionate about politics; however, dissenting views were not well tolerated. Strong opinions often flowed from both sides of an issue. It was not uncommon for friends to settle their differences like middle-school-aged children. In 1960, in Cuba, more than ever before, free speech was never truly free. More and more, dissenting views from established political leaders were considered hostile. Some Cubans admired the founding fathers of the United States and their establishment of the First Amendment of the Constitution. That right, in Cuba, was becoming just a dream to most. "The Yankees have their system, and we have ours," some said. Still, the ever-widening chasm of political vision for the future was not only alive and well but growing steadily.

Over the past year, Milva's father, Luis, had become increasingly withdrawn, and he hardly smiled anymore. He always seemed to stare off somewhere else. The revolution was changing him, along with many others who no longer recognized their Cuba. The country he had known was disintegrating before him. Despite the turmoil of the past, the nation still had respect, freedom of the press, private property, and open dialogue. One was even free to leave the country. However, to Luis Sr. and others, the present circumstances were becoming something they didn't recognize, were not prepared for, and did not want.

"The hostility goes beyond political disagreement," Luis Sr. said. "Friends and even family turn on one another. Betrayal, envy, and selfishness know no bounds. What are we becoming?"

Ciso's father, Felix, noticed the concerning changes as well. He was experiencing increased hostility from farmers who leased property from him and worked the land. The farmers lived in homes provided by him, and in exchange, they worked the tobacco fields and seasonal crops. "*Capitalista puerco!*" they would yell as he or his family drove by.

The Castro regime had begun seizing commercial and privately owned lands and properties belonging to wealthy individuals and businessmen. Those who had means and couldn't deal with their changing fortunes fled elsewhere with whatever they could. Even that was becoming a challenge. It was becoming increasingly difficult to leave the country. At first, most Cubans approved of the confiscation of property, thinking it would benefit everyone else—that was, themselves. However, those same Cubans slowly started turning on the regime over the next several months when the government came after the few possessions they had as well. Nothing was sacred. To a growing number of islanders, it was becoming all about the will of the state.

Ciso and Milva discussed much. She was mostly interested in his travel experiences in Europe. Milva's parents and her aunt Liche were eager to hear about his travels as well. Oswald, Milva's younger brother, sat quietly in his chair. Ciso said that although France was cold, it was exciting to see famous places, such as the Eiffel Tower and Champs-Élysées. Its open shops and sidewalk cafés were welcoming, and Ciso dreamed of a Cuba resembling France. He noticed that even after World War II, France had a growing and expanding economy, and that gave Ciso a vision of how things could be back home. Spain, on the other hand, was not as welcoming. He'd experienced disdain and an unfriendly attitude from the average Spaniard. He had known that would be the case, having heard from others who had been there before. "Cubanos are backward and stupid," many Spaniards had told him. No one in Spain lacked an opinion regarding the recent events taking place on the Caribbean island. "Castro is a visionary and a great man" seemed to be the consensus of many Spaniards with whom Ciso had met and spoken.

Milva listened, but she was more interested in famous landmarks she had been reading about since she was a girl than in politics. While in college, she'd majored in elementary education and read extensively on European civics and history. Now she taught in the small remote villages up in the hills of western Cuba near her town. Living rurally, in order to get to one particular school, she had to ride a mule because the roads were not conducive to cars.

Ciso laughed at her current mode of transportation, knowing how averse she was to outdoor life, let alone riding an animal. "I wish I could've seen that," he said, laughing.

She smiled from ear to ear as Ciso described many famous landmarks she had read about. "One day I've got to travel and experience it," she told him.

"*Es hora de comer*" (Time for dinner), said her mom, Micaela. The smell of black beans, fresh Cuban bread, and *palomilla* steak was overwhelming. Meat was becoming scarce, so it was a treat any time they could have it. Her father, Luis, the patriarch of their family, sat at the head of the table, dressed in his usual white cotton pants and white guayabera shirt.

The pleasantry of the afternoon was broken by the sound of vehicles pulling up the street and stopping in front of their house. Three men in green military uniforms hurried up the few short steps leading to the porch and banged on their front door, demanding that the owner of the home come forward. As Liche, Luis Sr.'s sister, opened the door, one of the men shoved her aside and walked right in, demanding that Luis Sr. identify himself and come forward. When he came forward, they grabbed him forcefully and dragged him out of the house toward one of their vehicles.

Upon seeing this, Milva nervously stood up and let out a cry. She recognized one of the armed uniformed men as a former college classmate. "What are you doing? Where are you taking my father?" she yelled with panic in her voice.

"He is to be questioned for not being in keeping with the revolution!" Lorenzo, her former classmate, scowled at her in response.

"You are mistaken. He has done nothing wrong. He—"

"*Callate la boca!*" Lorenzo said, interrupting her.

Milva, now in tears, joined her family, who were shocked. Her mother, Micaela, was visibly shaking in fear.

The other soldier in a green uniform, who had a black beard, overheard the conversation. He stepped into the doorway while a third soldier stayed with the car. "Listen here. We are going to make Cuba the Switzerland of the

Western Hemisphere." He proudly raised his right arm, waving his index finger in the air.

"Really?" cried Milva. "Look around! Where are the Swiss?"

Lorenzo and his bearded assistant turned around and forcefully escorted Luis, each holding him by one arm, and they drove off, leaving the family dismayed.

Just a few months earlier, Luis and Micaela had warned family and friends, including Ciso's family, of the dangers of the Marxist ideology and the ties to Castro that had infiltrated Cuba. *"No es posible"* was the common response. *"Castro promueve una Cuba libre con justicia social y mejorancia de la economía para todos."* Luis Sr. knew full well Castro did not promote freedom, justice, or economic improvement on the island. Many Cubans were slowly realizing how wrong they had been to buy into that party line and all their empty promises.

Milva and her mother, Micaela, cried, while Liche tried to comfort them, with little hope of her own. After a short while, they calmed down somewhat and tried to gather their thoughts. Liche seemed okay, but she was inwardly terrified at her brother Luis's predicament. The afternoon's events prompted her own memories from long ago.

Not long after she had finished her secondary education many years earlier, she had become engaged to Rene, a young man she had met at a church meeting.

Their friendship was immediate, and their attraction was swift. An idealistic youth, Rene was outspoken and intelligent, with a propensity to argue. Never shy or timid, he seemed to welcome and relish less popular beliefs. "Simple minds," he called the general populace. "Ill-informed and complacent, they receive what is given like *la cola de un perro*," he often told Liche. "Those who would have power lie, tell you what you want to hear, cause confusion, divide us, and divert our attention as they scheme and take what they can. And in the process, we applaud and blindly follow."

Liche, a small-town girl, was drawn to Rene's vigor, intelligence, and passion for life. She had never met anyone like him. They courted for almost a year. Rene was gone a lot, traveling mostly between Cuba and Argentina on communications business. "One day there will be a better and faster way to converse with others than telephone lines," he would tell her.

Just three months before their scheduled wedding, a small group of men approached Rene as he was walking to meet her in the late afternoon in town. There was a brief exchange of words, and a struggle ensued. In the encounter, Rene was shot and killed.

Chaos followed as the three men ran between the corner church and an old warehouse down the street. To make matters worse, Liche partially witnessed the event from her mother's flower shop just down the street. No one came forward, and no one was ever arrested. She never knew why he'd been killed, only that he was gone. There were rumors. Some said it had been an act of retribution; after all, Rene had been prone to confrontation. Others claimed the secret police were involved.

As the years passed, Liche did not give bitterness a foothold; however, the pain of that afternoon forever changed her. Many courters tried to win her hand over the years, but to no avail. Her true love was gone. She would never love another; being forever alone would have to do. As she clung to her faith, every time she passed that little church, she wondered why. Liche never married or allowed the completeness of companionship in love to rule her heart ever again.

Over the next few weeks, Ciso and Milva lobbied hard for Luis's return. Their efforts seemed futile. Her brother Luis Jr. was informed of the events two days later when he arrived from Havana. As the days passed, there was no sign of any progress. Then, to their astonishment, ten days after his arrest, Luis Sr. was released. Overall, he said, he hadn't been mistreated, despite the unpleasantness of the situation. However, he reported that several of his jail mates had met a different fate. Most were there because they had spoken out against the new regime, he said. "*No me gusta lo que está pasando!*" he told his family.

At the time, the family could not explain the release of Luis Sr. Was it justice? Possibly. Besides, he had done nothing wrong, Ciso said. "There is no crime in voicing your political opinion. Never has been. Not even under *el desgraciado* Batista." Still, it seemed odd to them. Luis Sr. had been openly outspoken about the dangers of Marxism and its similarities to the Castro regime. He had traveled abroad extensively and was well versed on political ideology. An avid reader, he often read his favorite writer, Blasco Ibáñez, who wrote of the ways of the West and of Asia. They found it perplexing that the new regime had released him so quickly, when others just as easily perished.

Over the next few weeks, Ciso and Milva's brother Luis Jr lobbied hard for Luis' return. Two weeks later, he was released. Overall, his treatment was not too difficult. However, he reported several of his jail mates met a different fate. "Most were there because they had spoken against the new regime. Que esta pasando?" he often wondered. Years later, Ciso and Milva learned that Luis Jr had somehow successfully procured the release of their father when he had been arrested. Just a few weeks after Batista had fled the country, her brother was medically treating the locals of a small town somewhere in western Cuba. Late one evening, he was awoken and informed that a high-ranking official was about to arrive at any moment in need of medical attention. Several minutes later, a small armada of vehicles pulled up to the small country clinic. Once Luis Jr had introduced himself, a man in his twenties with a dark short beard followed several guards and identified himself as Che Guevarra. Suffering from an apparent asthma attack, he needed a breathing treatment that the clinic happened to have on hand. While being treated, Guevarra spoke candidly and kindly to Luis Jr. "Don't worry Doc, you have nothing to fear from me. You know, I'm a doctor too. Besides, your services will soon be in ever increasing demand." Small talk ensued. Luis Jr had heard there was a rumor that an order was given by Fidel that if the Americans were to invade, all prisoners would be executed. "Comandante, es verdad?" he asked him. Che cautioned Luis Jr to be careful and avoid jail at all cost and that if he ran into any trouble, to mention his name. The high official thanked him for the breathing treatment and just as quickly they arrived, he and his entourage continued on their journey. Now a year later, Luis Jr had made a few phone calls while Luis Sr was incarcerated and most assuredly saved his father's life.

Later that year, Ciso and Milva were married in a simple ceremony in their hometown. They moved into Milva's parents' house, and Ciso worked with his father delivering cigars and produce with the family business. Over the next several months, commodities were harder to come by, and the means to produce them were increasingly difficult. Government restrictions and endless regulations were starting to choke their enterprise. Ciso tried to stay optimistic. His father, Felix, was anything but.

Twelve months later, Milva miscarried their first child. Ciso took the news hard and went into the hills of western Cuba for three days alone. Milva had the support of her family but needed him. She understood his way of dealing with grief, yet she felt left out of her husband's deep emotional world, which she felt she should've been a part of.

When he returned, they resumed married life, now changed by the impact of such a loss. Milva did the best she could to put the loss behind her as she forced herself to look toward the future. She said, "The pain of this loss we will have to carry with us forever, but we must give him and the pain to God and let—"

"Stop! Don't speak to me about God. Where was he when we needed him most? You carried that child for nine months, and all was fine, only for him to be born dead. *Muerto*! Why? A beautiful little boy. Our boy." Ciso's face reddened as he tried desperately to hold at bay a torrential display of hurt that deep loss brought. His eyes held back their tears for now.

Milva stood looking toward a photograph on the end table of her oldest sister gone long ago. She looked back to Ciso. "*Dia por dia*, we will get through this."

Ciso carried that burden deep in his heart yet refused to talk any more about it. The deep hurt of losing his firstborn son gave way to anger and frustration. Ultimately, their intimacy took a backseat to necessity. Milva felt there was a rift between them and thought it would take only a matter of time to heal.

A year later, their daughter, Margret, was born. She was a healthy and beautiful baby. Milva's pregnancy was tolerable, as she described later. In the fall of 1962, she was pregnant again. This time, while in her second trimester, she experienced heavy hemorrhaging brought on by an Rh incompatibility with the new baby. Her brother Luis Jr., a well-established and respected physician in the community, was determined to save the child. He insisted she be on bed rest for the last three months of her pregnancy as he administered vitamin K injections regularly. In March 1963, little Quintin came into the world, barely. The delivery was difficult but successful.

Ciso didn't know what to make of his new son. "What is wrong with him?" he asked with great concern. The child weighed in at ten pounds, was green with jaundice, and had been born with an inverted right ankle, which required a rudimentary orthotic shoe and a foot brace for the first few years of his life.

Milva slowly recovered, and several days later, they returned home. They continued to share their two-bedroom home with her parents, her aunt Liche, and Milva's younger brother, Oswald.

Over the next few short years, Ciso tried to make sense of his changing nation. The events on the bus from the airport, the growing scarcity of basic provisions, the lack of free press, and the growing hostility of the people, especially neighbors, made him increasingly uneasy. There was also a general sense of uncertainty, and his father-in-law and others had been arrested without just cause. *What is going on?* he thought. He and others dreamed of a free, democratic, and prosperous Cuba centered on a constitution. It appeared to him the country was headed in the opposite direction. The vision he, his friends, and many others had of self-governance and a free, independent Cuba was insidiously fading.

CHAPTER 6

Candidates, Fall 1986

The experiences in Aviation Officer Candidate School (AOCS) were profound and life-changing. It was said the weeks went by like days, and the days were like weeks. Two and a half months had passed since the initial hell week, and the adaptive misery of those days was on Quintin's mind. *Four weeks to go, and I'll be a commissioned officer in the US Navy. Yeah, baby.*

Fifty-two officer candidates had begun that challenge, and only eleven of the original candidates remained. Many of the candidates had dropped on request (DOR) or been held back due to medical issues. Several new faces were added from previous classes for various reasons, mostly medical.

"Girls, in a few days, you will be in survival training," said Gunny. "Till then, attention! Dress right, dress. Ready. Two."

Like little soldiers lined up on a board game, they were preparing for the daily three-mile formation run.

"Right face!"

As if one, the candidates turned ninety degrees to the right, all except candidate Gronski. Taller and heavier than most, he was less coordinated in precision of bodily movements, and it was obvious. To the drill instructor's disdain, he had been struggling with precision marching and rifle drills and was no stranger to "On your face."

"Gronski! You moron, what is it with you? This is not a hip-swinging dance contest. Get your ass out of formation, and get to the back. I'll deal with you later."

Poor bastard, thought Quintin. *I don't know why he is still here. How much verbal abuse can a guy take?*

The day went as usual. They marched into chow, had their classes in the afternoon and further academic tests, and had more rifle drills with their M1 Garand carbines. There was a bit of a break after the evening chow when they studied the day's lessons and interacted with fellow classmates.

"Hey, Quintin, you think you're ready for survival?" asked Jessie.

"Oh, heck yeah," answered Quintin. "Should be all right. You?"

Jessie was the son of watermelon farmers in Alabama. Quintin wasn't used to his southern ways yet felt at ease with him. Jessie's blond hair had been growing—like everyone else's—since the first week. Hair length was a good indicator of which class a person was in during the fourteen weeks. He was a good ole boy, and Quintin had come to respect and befriend him.

"I reckon so," Jessie casually responded.

Quintin thought his buddy's farm life might not have

prepared him for survival training. Still, he hoped his friend would surprise him.

Then there was John Willsby. John had formerly enlisted with the navy and now was training to become an officer. He knew more than a little about the man's navy and probably understood the rigors and purposes of the place better than most of the candidates. Over time, Quintin couldn't figure out how Willsby got away with repeated infractions. Whether it was language, proper uniform wearing, or marching, good ole Willsby never seemed to raise the fury of the drill instructors. Quintin often wondered, *How the hell does he get away with it?* They were always under the watchful eyes of the DIs. When Quintin didn't wear his cover—appropriate head covering—the drill instructor caught him for being out of uniform and put him on his face, along with many of his classmates. On the other hand, one afternoon, Willsby showered but forgot his towel in his room. He took off running to the other side of the barracks through the main hall, butt naked, screaming, "Geronimo!" All the candidates laughed at the moment but were shocked that he never got caught. *Hmm*, Quintin thought. *He must know something we don't.*

The class was fairly tight, as they had gotten to know each other pretty well during the previous ten weeks. Being pushed to their limits mentally, emotionally, and physically caused the candidates to be dependent on one other. "Teamwork—a way of life, sir" was often repeated as required by the candidates in response to the DIs when group effort was demanded. That didn't keep them from being fiercely competitive, however. Each thought he was better than anyone else in the class, yet they maintained mutual respect. That was part of stripping down and building up the navy way.

One of the most impactful exercises was survival training. The class was broken into groups of twelve, which included members from other military services. For two days, the instructors taught the age-old activities of foraging, smoking meat, gathering wood for fires, looking for water, and so on. The camp was located about two hours away in a remote area of the Florida Panhandle. It was a welcome break from the endless routine of drills, marches, and studying. During the evening, the temperature out in the woods dropped down to the forties, and a simple flight suit and boots were not enough to keep them warm. *Maybe being back in the battalion is not such a bad idea*, Quintin thought.

On the first night of survival training, at dusk, a large fire was started in the middle of Quintin's twelve-man group under the canopy of trees. The fire helped tremendously, even though the ground felt so cold it chilled their bones. Each member dug a small hole big enough to fit into and deep enough to shield from the open air. They tried to dig close enough to the fire without getting cooked. Quintin had to turn every fifteen minutes to warm different parts of his body. The drastic difference in temperature kept him and the others from quality sleep, as the side touching the ground grew cold and painful, and the side toward the fire was warm and toasty. As if they were human rotisseries, the turning lasted throughout the night.

"Hey, Joey," said one of the aviation crewmen in the group. "You know what I would love to have right about now?"

"No, what?" said Joey, another candidate several feet away, in a low, exhausted tone.

"A great big pizza. New York style."

Quintin was pretty sure the others' thoughts were like his. He was thinking about warm, melted mozzarella cheese with pepperoni, sausage, or ham—it didn't matter as long as it had lots of warm grease. They hadn't eaten anything of substance in almost two days. They did, however, have plenty of water. The navy made sure everyone was hydrated. Everything else was secondary. Showers, food, comfort, and even brushing one's teeth were luxuries not to be had.

There was minimal conversation throughout the evening. Each member present just endured and went on.

"Hey, Joey, I wish I had a large pot of hot coffee and my girl—"

"Shut the hell up, asshole!" said Willsby. "If you open

your mouth again, I'm gonna put my foot up your ass!" Nobody disagreed with that plan of action, including Quintin. No one else uttered a word. It was time to turn again.

The following day began with more training and survival skills. With hunger ever present, they opted to hunt in the forest for a small animal they could catch, kill, and eat, perhaps a rabbit or squirrel—it didn't matter. It was no small task, given that no one had any weapons other than a standard-issue knife, and most of them had no experience in hunting.

It wasn't long before the group spotted and were able to surround an armadillo. Quintin thought, *This is gonna be a piece of cake.*

"Dinner bell is ringing, boys!" said one of the twelve.

As the circle closed in on the unfortunate prey, the poor creature seemed, at least to Quintin, to be in a dire predicament. As the poor creature looked around for an escape route, it quickly realized there was none to be had. The creature, surrounded on all sides by the apex human predators, must've realized its doomed destiny. Sensing a trap, it looked in several different directions without any obvious escape route. Suddenly, it seemed to focus on the tall air force candidate directly to Quintin's right. Each member stopped and seemed to hold his breath in a moment of hesitation as the situation unfolded. Without any warning, the creature darted for him, and when it was about four feet from its target, it jumped into the air and struck the poor guy in the chest.

A loud scream came from the supposed fearless warrior as he tried to bat the creature away, almost falling backward in the process. Seconds later, the armadillo was free from the circle of death and disappeared into the brush. The candidates were left speechless, feeling deflated, defeated, and still quite hungry. No one said a word for at least an hour.

Later that afternoon, about an hour before sundown, one of the instructors came by to check on them. "You guys look about as pathetic as anyone I've ever seen. Leave your stuff where it is, and follow me."

He led them to one of the other nearby encampments, where several candidates from Quintin's class were. Quintin recognized Jessie cleaning something in the small stream. "Jessie, what's going on?" he asked.

"Well, take a look. We caught him several hours ago. This is gonna be our dinner," he responded. It looked like a small animal about the size of a house cat, only it was missing its organs and outer skin.

"You guys caught an armadillo?"

"Yep," Jessie said with half a smile.

Quintin had never seen an armadillo without its shell and internal organs. It reminded him of an alien creature, like something out of science fiction, hideously ugly and not appetizing.

Jessie and several of his camp mates also had built a small net with fishing line they had found and had trapped several small brook trout in a nearby stream that led to a small lake. "We're gonna have a feast tonight," said one from their group.

Quintin's mates returned to their camp for the last evening of their survival training. *It pays to know how to be resourceful and live off the land*, Quintin thought. He was impressed that Jessie had the necessary skills, despite his previous doubts.

That night, like the one before, was bitterly cold. The thought of several other classmates going to bed on a full stomach made the night even colder. *Sure will be glad when this is over*, Quintin thought as he tried to get comfortable in his dirt hole. *If nothing else, to at least take a hot shower and brush my teeth.* He closed his eyes. It was time to turn again.

CHAPTER 7

The Lottery, 1968

"*Atencion*! *Atencion*! Numbers 2125, 2022, and 1517, gather yourselves, and come to the administrative office."

Lucky bastards, thought Ciso. Six months had passed at the work camp since he had applied for asylum to the USA. He and several hundred men had been informed they had to report to a manual labor camp at one of the government-run farms in order to obtain an exit visa to leave Cuba. *No luck today*, thought Ciso. He would have to wait another week, when they would select the next set of numbers.

He sat down in the large mess hall, and one by one, each row of workers got up to take their turn in the food line for their evening meal. Amid the heat, humidity, mosquitoes, and flies, life went on in that epic little corner of western Cuba.

"*Apurate*!" barked the uniformed attendant as he held out a large spoonful of the daily broth.

"I wonder what the mystery meat today is," Ciso said out loud.

"Don't look at it so much. Just eat it!" replied Lipio. His old friend had gotten to the work camp several weeks after Ciso and didn't seem to mind the offerings of their new hosts.

Lipio was no stranger to hardship. His childhood had been difficult, and the constant search for basic necessities was ongoing.

With the revolution now firmly in Castro's hands, there had been drastic changes on the island over the past eight years. Provisions, such as food, building materials, and clothing, were becoming increasingly scarce. Ciso and others worried about the future for their country, themselves, and especially their children. Amid the lack of necessities, coupled with the lack of liberties, Ciso had made the difficult decision to expatriate and leave his beloved Cuba. Many others felt the same, and the government work camps were becoming ever more numerous. Year after year, he had been certain they could weather the economic difficulties; however, the lack of freedom was the final straw. The Soviet Union was increasingly supporting the new government and tightening its grip on the island nation. However, the economy was increasingly stagnated. Outspoken civil liberties were not tolerated, and speedy trials and rapid sentencing were becoming the norm. *How the hell did we get here?* thought Ciso.

His thoughts turned to Milva and his two young children. Margret was now seven, and Quintin, his miracle son, was an active five-year-old.

"*Cometelo*!" Lipio said once again.

They glanced at each other and ate their chowder, not seeming to mind the one or two maggots in their local offering. Ciso was glad to have Lipio by his side. He was a childhood friend and had been partly raised by Ciso's parents, Felix and Margo. He had been unofficially adopted by them at a young age. Life had made him tough, resilient, and resourceful. If Huckleberry Finn had had a Spanish twin, Lipio could have worn the shoes.

Lipio's father was a Spaniard who had abandoned him and his mother and returned to Spain shortly after Lipio was born. His mother had tried to raise him with little family support. She'd succumbed to fever and died when he was only five. Since Lipio and Ciso had been born at about the same time, as infants, they'd had the same wet nurse. Neither one of their biological mothers had been able to nurse her newborn. Negra Juana, as the wet nurse was called, had given birth to her sixth child and offered her services to feed both boys. Juana had served as a wet nurse for many babies in their region. Years later, Juana often told Ciso that as an infant, he would latch on easily and feed with such ferocity he would emerge profusely sweating. He always blushed when the subject was brought up, but he was grateful for her life-giving generosity. In rural Cuba during the 1930s, their needs had been real and unforgiving. Many regions had endured however they could during those difficult years.

As time dragged on, the weekly numbers were read, and not one of Ciso's numbers matched. *O cara, is this rigged?* he wondered. Some of the men were there for only a couple of weeks before their numbers were called.

The day-to-day activities at the camp were monotonous and routine, but some days involved backbreaking work in the fields. They weren't forced to stay, but they had no chance of an exit visa if they left. Word reached the camp that some brave souls had attempted to steal boats or stow away on barges or small canoes to cross the Florida Straits, hoping to make it to the United States. No one ever found out if any of them actually made it.

Ciso's father would visit whenever he could. His mother had come down with early advanced Parkinson's, which made walking difficult for her. In addition to tremors, Margo experienced delayed speech, and she was physically slowing down rapidly. While in her thirties, she'd had one breast removed due to cancer. Now, in her late fifties, she was fighting for basic activities of daily living. Medications were increasingly scarce, but whenever she was able to come across them, she responded relatively well.

Felix was well known and respected in the territory. The second oldest of ten sons with two younger sisters, he was quiet, stubborn, and business savvy. He had been born on the family's kitchen table, a common occurrence in those days, in 1904. He spent his preschool years mostly helping around the farm. He loved reading; however, he left school in the fourth grade in order to help feed his family. His parents needed help running the farm, and since Felix was the second oldest, he was sorely needed.

Charismatic, smart, and good looking, he was a force to reckon with. He appeared to have endless energy, which made him a favorite to handle the family's affairs. That did not sit well with his older brother, Ramon. Early on, the boys settled their differences by coming to blows. Later, Felix came to distrust Ramon, and Ramon wasted no time in demeaning his younger brother at every opportunity. Although Felix often said he didn't hold grudges, once he crossed someone off, it was done, blood or not. The two brothers eventually tolerated each other, as demanded by their father. However, sometimes there was nothing worse than a crime of the heart.

At nineteen, Ramon met a young girl named Sira, and the two began seeing each other when Ramon and Felix's father made trips to buy goods in town. Ramon was taken by her, and eventually, her parents allowed Ramon to visit her from time to time but only under the eye of a chaperone.

On one Sunday afternoon, Ramon came into town, riding on the back of a neighbor's truck. Ramon's father was to pick him up later in the afternoon. However, his father was installing a hand pump on a well on their farm and asked Felix to go fetch Ramon instead. Felix arrived at Sira's house and introduced himself to her, the chaperone, and Sira's little sister. His good looks, with curly black hair and a tan and toned body, did not go unnoticed. Sira tried not to stare. Felix felt her presence as well. The obvious attraction between them made everyone uncomfortable, especially Ramon.

The ride back to their home was quiet; neither brother said a word. Their already estranged relationship only grew further apart.

Several days later, Felix visited Sira one late evening. She quietly came outside, this time alone. He'd brought her a handful of gardenias, and they spoke quietly to each other. Sira was flirtatious, and their attraction was mutual. With little time to lose, he embraced and kissed her. However, she stopped him when he tried to unbutton her blouse.

"No, *no puedo*," she said.

He tried again, and this time, he met little resistance.

When Felix returned home that night, Ramon glared at his brother. The two had reached a point of no return.

In 1921, with a keen eye for opportunity, Felix started his trucking business using a small truck at the age of seventeen. The truck had no cabin and had a gas tank as the driver's seat. All his siblings worked for him, except Ramon. Felix was driven and devoted to whatever task was at hand. Known to have a wicked temper, he developed the virtue of patience as the years passed. Slowly, he began to build a name for himself. After balancing the overhead expenses and paying his growing number of employees, he invested what was left over in his many ventures. There was one word not in his vocabulary: *vacation.* "Waste of time. That which does not produce is irrelevant and no good," he said.

After initially planting vegetables, he quickly expanded to fruit and eventually tobacco. Although he was frugal and determined, success in the late 1920s and '30s came slowly. He built his home not far from his parents' house, just off the main road, with easy access to fields and highways to facilitate the transport of goods. He called his farm el Retiro (the Retirement).

Felix's visits to the government work camp always gave Ciso reassurance. He would bring news of Margo's health and updates on Ciso's wife, Milva, and the children.

"You know, you don't have to do this," said his father. "I have lived through tough times before and done well. As long as we keep the family together, we will be okay. Besides, *el Comunismo* won't last long. It doesn't make any sense, and the Americans won't tolerate it being ninety miles from their borders."

Ciso was in deep thought as he eyed his aging father. The regime had been in power for eight years, and he thought the future of the island was increasingly bleak. "*Viejo*, where did we go wrong? Fidel spoke of change, justice, and equality. I'm not seeing any of it."

"You'd better keep your mouth shut," Lipio said. "If our uniformed hosts hear you, you might disappear just like many others have for saying less. Besides, you don't know who is listening. Anyone might be desperate enough to turn us in to gain favors."

News had gotten out that political dissenters were treated harshly. According to stories, even one of Fidel's inner circle had gone missing after getting on a flight with a few officials and their security details. When the plane landed, he never deplaned. He was never seen again.

Lipio gave Felix a firm handshake and a wide smile. Felix felt he was visiting not one but two sons. Lipio, always jovial no matter the circumstance, could have been the world's answer to depression. As he started one of his predictable and never-ending supply of jokes, Ciso cut him off before he could get the second word out of his mouth. Felix just stared quietly, rolling the cigar in his mouth. "*Ahora no, coño,*" said Ciso angrily.

Lipio ignored him and proceeded to tell the joke anyway.

"*O cara,*" responded Ciso.

The weeks seemed like months to some in the camp, but it felt like years to Ciso. Day after day, the men worked the fields, loaded the few trucks that were running, and transported farm goods to distribution centers in Cuba. He got to know a mix of rural and urban workers. To those with farming backgrounds, the government's distribution and planting of crops as well as raising of domestic animals made no sense. The decisions the regime made regarding the needed goods did not seem to coincide with market demands. Some crops were ordered to be planted only to fail because it was the wrong season. The domestic animals that were prioritized had no bearing on the needs or wants of the general population or market demands for exporting. Some regions and farmers were told which crops or animals they were to raise. There was a constant demand for beef, yet cattle farmers were ordered to raise something else. Frustration and fatigue often gave way to anger and apathy. Theft, once uncommon, was rising in the urban and rural areas. Some farmers even secretly started raising pigs or chickens in the bathrooms of their homes.

Just when Ciso didn't think he could take much more, in mid-November 1968, his lottery number was finally called.

Lipio was the first to congratulate his heart brother. "I've been praying for you—and me, for that matter—to leave this place," he said as he stared at Ciso with his usual wide smile. "You have two young children I love, so it's fitting that you should go first."

"Praying! What will that do?"

"God answered my prayer. Don't you see it?" responded Lipio, still smiling.

Processing the exit papers in the current bureaucracy would take several days. Working in the fields those last few days didn't feel like such a burden any longer. Finally, with exit visa in hand, Ciso, now thirty-four years old, was free to leave the country. The responses from his fellow workers were a combination of well-wishes and envy, considering their own plights. A few had been there as long as two years.

Lipio wasn't as fortunate; he remained there for another four months. Later, he recounted, the conditions at the camp worsened. Basic necessities were increasingly scarce, guards were bribed for favors, and the Cuban government cracked down even more severely on political dissent and granted fewer exit visas. Even Lipio's seemingly unending jovial demeanor was tested. The once talkative, happy-go-lucky hillbilly rarely spoke of those months in the years that followed.

Once Ciso reached home, his father's farm was a welcome sight. The next few days seemed to fly by. They were preparing to fly to Los Angeles, California. Ciso, Milva, and their two children were sponsored by Milva's aunt, who had lived there since the early 1950s. They packed minimal belongings and said goodbye to a few close neighbors. Preparing to leave was emotional and trying. Ciso's parents Felix and Margo as well as Milva's parents Luis Sr. and Micaela accompanied them with their two children, seven-year-old Margaret and five-year-old Quintin to the Havana airport.

The drive to the airport was tense and quiet. When

they arrived, silence gave way to hugs and tears. Three generations were on hand. The oldest held the youngest a little longer. At the final call, Felix told his son Ciso once again, "You know, you don't have to go. We can stay together and make it work, no matter how bad things get." Family meant everything to *Abuelo* Felix.

"I'm not raising my kids without freedom," responded Ciso. Things were not looking encouraging on the island. There was a rumor that a law had been passed declaring all males eight years or older would not be permitted to leave the country, presumably to be indoctrinated at school and then forced into obligatory military service. Ciso gave his father a knowing look. He had to go for the sake of his young children.

Ciso and his family boarded the DC-3 aircraft while the grandparents as well as other nearby families watched their loved ones board. Tears flowed. With her emotions taking over, Micaela fell to her knees. Luis appeared deadpan and emotionless, obscuring a deep pain and sorrow he would never recover from. It was said he never smiled again. "He gave up on life," those close to him often said. The man who'd started and run a social club and been known for fun and happiness could take no more. The sight of his little girl leaving and taking his grandchildren with her was more than he could bear. Just a few short years later, he passed away quietly, more than likely from deep sadness and a broken heart.

Micaela tried to keep it together for her oldest child, Luis Jr., and his family, who were unable to leave due to his status as a physician. Her youngest son, Oswald, needed her the most, as his autism made him completely dependent on her for his needs. Leaving the country was never an option for Luis and Micaela. With the country's newly implemented policies, medical professionals and individuals with special needs were not permitted to leave Cuba. That anchored Luis Jr. and Micaela.

Felix kept it together but just barely. He knew the likelihood of ever seeing his loved ones again was grim. Five years later, he suffered a heart attack. While he initially recovered at a nearby rural clinic, that evening, his nurse heard him say, "*Donde esta mi gente?*"

He did not survive the second heart attack that evening. He died alone without any family present. News of his final words reached Ciso, who was now in Miami, the following day, and the news hit him hard. He would spend the rest of his life second-guessing his decision to flee Cuba for the sake of his children, leaving behind his parents, his vulnerable siblings, and their way of life for the sake of freedom.

CHAPTER 8

The Boat, Summer 1987

"Buckeye 211, you are cleared for takeoff."

"Roger, Tower. Buckeye 211 is clear for takeoff."

One by one, each of the T-2C Buckeye trainer jets took off from Boca Chica Naval Air Station in Key West, Florida. It was midday, with plenty of sun and a light breeze blowing out of the southeast on a warm December afternoon in 1987. The flight leader was an instructor only a couple of years older than Quintin. He was in charge of leading three fledgling naval aviator students. Anticipation was high, which slowly gave way to nervous energy during their flight. As all four twin-engine jet trainers rendezvous in formation after takeoff, the flight turned northwest and headed out to open sea. This was it: after a full year spent in the naval air training command, everything they had done had led to this moment. This was what they had been training for: carrier landing qualifications.

Quintin had spent the first six months at NAS Whiting Field outside Pensacola, Florida. It was Quintin's first experience in flying. After four weeks of intense ground school, the students were introduced to the air by their assigned instructors. Takeoffs, landings, navigation, communication, emergency procedures, and formation flying were on the syllabus, and each student was expected to master each task before moving on to the next. The T-34 Mentor turboprop was the navy's primary flight trainer. *What a fun aircraft to fly,* Quintin thought. Primary flight training was fast-paced and involved extensive daily flight preparation, with rigorous course rules, regulations, and aircraft systems. He spent most of the evening hours studying. Quintin chose to live on base at the bachelor officer quarters (BOQ) to stay focused. Some of his classmates lived off base in one of the many nearby apartments or townhomes. *Too many distractions,* he thought. Too often, the students who lived off base tended to rendezvous at the nearest bar, meet ladies, and light their hair on fire. Quintin wanted to stay focused on his training. Besides, his thoughts were of Cari back home. *I miss her, but it's good she's not here. Having her here would be too much of a distraction. There will be time enough for that.* He focused on memorizing the emergency procedures for fire in flight.

Pensacola was a well-known navy town and was known as the cradle of US naval aviation. In January 1911, a civilian pilot named Eugene Ely had made the first landing on a ship called the USS *Pennsylvania* in San Francisco Bay. After almost landing in the water while attempting to do the same several months earlier in Hampton Roads, Virginia, Ely wrapped himself with inflated inner tubes to use as flotation devices. Unfortunately, the young civilian daredevil lost his life in October of that year during a demonstration flight in Georgia.

The first naval aviators had arrived in Pensacola in 1914. At the start of World War I, the navy's first and only air station had three dozen aviators and approximately fifty-four fixed-wing aircraft. Flight training slowed down right after the war, and real interest in training didn't resume until 1935. World War II started for the United States with the carrier-launched air attack on Pearl Harbor by the Japanese Imperial Navy. From then on, carriers dominated the Pacific theater.

One of Quintin's officer candidate school (OCS) classmates was his next-door neighbor at the BOQ.

"Hey, Ensign Jessie, don't know about you, but I'm ready to start flying!" Quintin said when his buddy came over to see him. The ground school portion was over, and flights were about to begin.

Jessie didn't answer. These former candidates were now commissioned officers in the United States Navy. There were three primary flight training squadrons at Whiting Field. The airfield was located in Milton, just northeast of Pensacola, Florida. Jessie was assigned to one of the other squadrons, and he'd had some difficulties in adjusting to the following phases on their way to becoming naval aviators.

"Hey, do you ever have any doubts?" asked Jessie.

"Doubts? What doubts?" replied Quintin.

"Doubts about going through with all of this: first AOCS and now flight school, followed by intermediate and advanced training in jets and, later, long deployments."

"Nah, dude, I've wanted to fly jets since I was a kid. My dad wanted me to go into construction with him. Tried that. Forget it. I've got too much piss and vinegar running through my veins."

"Did you tell me before that your family were farmers?" asked Jessie.

"Yeah, my grandfather grew tobacco and sold cigars way back in Cuba. Why do you ask?"

"You don't like farming, Quintin? Where I come from, there's nothing like open spaces, trees, and streams. My daddy made a business of growing and selling melons on our one hundred ten acres."

Quintin stared at Jessie, wondering where the conversation was going. "Dude, we just went through fourteen weeks of hell, and now we're in flight school. What are you saying?"

Jessie, looking out the window, reflected for a moment. "I'm heading home. This is not for me. I'd like to get back to the farm. I proved to myself I could make it, and I did. I just don't think I'm cut out for this life."

It would be several years before Quintin realized that Jessie had made the right decision. *If your heart's not in this business, it's best to move on to something else before you get yourself or someone else killed*, Quintin concluded. Still, he would miss that hillbilly.

The four twin-engine jets climbed to sixteen thousand feet and leveled off. Quintin was second plane, or dash-two, as it was called, while his other two classmates' call signs, Rodent and Gunther, were dash-three and dash-four. They'd completed preflight briefing and run through the required checklists. All aviators lived and died by the checklist. Strict adherence to the checklist as well as the naval operations manual procedures was doctrine. If pilots violated them, they would pay dearly, maybe even with their lives. In aviation, rules were written in blood.

Rodent was from Rhode Island and dreamed of flying the A-6 Intruder, the navy's carrier-based attack bomber. Gunther was a marine from Ohio. He was hell-bent on F-18 Hornets. "Although Harrier jump jets would do as well," he said. All three students needed to be carrier qualified before moving on to advanced jets, such as the A-4 Skyhawk.

In the backseat of the lead aircraft was a naval academy student going along for the experience of her life. Wisely, the instructor was the only pilot allowed a passenger. The three students were considered too dangerous, and if they screwed up, it was better for there to be only one casualty rather than two.

As Quintin tried to relax in his seat, he flew loose

formation off the flight lead and dialed in the ship's navigation channel for distance and bearing to the aircraft carrier. Thirty-two miles was the indicated range to the ship. There was blue ocean as far as the eye could see, and scant clouds with unlimited visibility was the present weather. Flying over the ocean, or what the navy called "feet wet," was like stepping into a different world. The beautiful shades of turquoise, green, and blue of the sea made it hard to keep one's eyes off it. The student pilots had been training for carrier landings since starting flight school, which had included hundreds of field carrier landing practices (FCLPs) at home base in Meridian, Mississippi.

All three students flew loose formation, and as Quintin settled in, he felt calm and eager to join the Tailhooker Club. *This is not so bad*, he thought. *So far so good. We're not just pilots but aviators—best of the best. I can do this. No sweat.* In any case, looking bad was a fate worse than death. He quickly scanned his instruments—oil pressure, attitude, fuel—and then went back to eyes out and maintained formation. A midair collision would have ruined everyone's day.

Their flight took them on a northwesterly heading into the Gulf of Mexico. He could see a few whitecaps on the ocean surface. *Fifteen to twenty knots of wind*, he estimated. As the distance to the carrier indicated six miles, he took a quick glance at the ocean ahead to get a glimpse of the ship. Every once in a while, Quintin could see the female cadet in the backseat of the instructor glance back at the other three jets. *I wonder what she's thinking,* he thought. *Ah, she's probably in wonder at how awesome we are. She's gotta be impressed—no doubt about it.* Quintin was starting to feel confident by then as he continued looking for the ship. *Where is she? Where is that big mama?* he thought as he scanned the ocean below. He was looking for a huge ship. *Why can't I see her?*

Suddenly, the ship appeared as if out of thin air. "Tally Ho! There she is." *Oh crap!* His mind snapped back. The enormous ship he was looking for appeared tiny in the enormity of the surrounding ocean. Almost a thousand feet of floating steel looked like a tiny gray piece of driftwood. His thoughts started to race, his heart pounded faster, and he started breathing so fast that he thought he might pass out while 100 percent oxygen flowed through his mask. *Settle down,* he kept telling himself. As he glanced at his squadron buddies in aircraft three and four, it was obvious they were crapping in their pants too. Their tight formation flying had seriously deteriorated since they spotted *Lady Lex,* as the carrier was often called. *A flock of pelicans would be ashamed of this formation,* he thought.

They kept radio silence, only letting the flight lead communicate, so as not to overwhelm the airwaves. The USS *Lexington* was a legendary World War II aircraft carrier. She was the second ship to carry the name, as the first had been lost in the Battle of the Coral Sea in 1942. That sea battle had been the first time in naval history when opposing ships never saw each other; the battle had raged among aircraft. The newly commissioned *Lex* had established herself in the western Pacific, taking kamikaze hits in the final days of the war, and eventually numerous deployments all over the world in the years that followed. At present, she was used as the navy's training platform for future naval aviators.

"Stay in formation. Tighten it up," the flight lead said over the radio.

Stick to the training, thought Quintin. Anxiety gave way to downright fear. *What the hell am I doing? I don't know if I can do this.* Fear seemed to take over his mind and emotions. He did not know which one would dominate the moment, but he felt totally alone. From one unknown section of his mind, he heard, *Concentrate, damn it.* From other areas, he heard, *Get the hell out of here, or you will die!*

Mr. Fear said, *I'm going to crash and burn!*

I'm crapping in my pants! was the message voiced from deep emotion.

By then, his legs were shaking so much that his feet were bouncing off the rudder pedals. *Oh crap! I am going to die! This is nuts.* His thoughts raced faster and faster. *Settle down*, he kept telling himself.

With sweat pouring, body shaking, and mind in hyperspeed, he heard a calm, deep voice come over his headset: "Buckeyes Charlie." That was the signal from the carrier's air boss to leave the holding pattern and begin the landing sequence. The air boss ruled the airspace several miles from the ship. The role of air boss went to an experienced naval aviator, and he was to be obeyed at all costs. God help pilots who didn't.

Quintin muttered, *Lord, if you get me through this, I'll ...*

They flew in formation as best as they could, given their inexperience. The flight lead led them down along the starboard—right side—of the ship to the break where each aircraft would turn hard left away from the formation in fifteen-second intervals upwind. Things are happening even faster now. They were accelerating and in close parade formation—sort of.

Remember the procedures, damn it. Fly the aircraft, he thought. He could see the naval cadet student occasionally look back, and he later wondered what was going through her mind at that moment. The only thing going through his mind was *Please, Lord, don't let me screw this up! I don't want to die, but don't let me look bad.*

Down they went, the flight lead with three fledglings. It was time to stroke those fictitious egos or crash and burn. If there was one thing the pilots cared about, it was who the best pilot was. If one wanted to fly fighters, he had to shine, especially at the boat.

As they flew up the right side of the carrier, Quintin could see her gray figure and island structure in his peripheral vision. He dared not take his eyes off the lead. Several hundred feet in front of *Lady Lex*, the flight leader kissed off and banked hard left, almost ninety degrees, to begin the landing sequence. Fifteen seconds later, Quintin did the same, and so on. As he rolled to an eighty-degree angle of bank, with throttles to idle, he pulled back on the stick to maintain eight hundred feet above sea level; the airspeed quickly bled off. He scanned the instruments, and training took over: *At the appropriate airspeed, landing gear down, deploy flaps, scan angle of attack, descend to altitude of six hundred feet, check spacing and distance from the ship, and scan, scan, scan.* He went through each item on the memorized landing checklist. Now on downwind, the ship was coming toward them from the left side. The maneuver was going to be two hookup landings called touch-and-gos, with no arrestment. It required total and complete concentration, as things were happening even faster now. As he flew his aircraft, he continually quickly scanned his instruments, making adjustments on attitude, throttles, angle of attack, speed, distancing, and other metrics pertaining to the aircraft and its location in that piece of the sky in relation to the ship. He was still shaking and anxious, and the pucker factor—a term pilots used to describe the anal opening—was high. The more stress there was, the tighter it was. There was never a shortage of acronyms or nicknames in naval air.

At what was called the abeam—across the stern of the ship 180 degrees in the opposite direction—Quintin started a gentle thirty-degree angle of bank left turn and then a slow descent. Each position of the landing sequence was all about precision; he made slow and small corrections as he dealt with the multiple inputs coming into his brain. Large corrections were obvious, dangerous, and synonymous with getting behind the aircraft, a position not conducive to surviving, let alone looking good. Again and again, he scanned his speed, angle of attack, descent rate, position, and throttles. *So far so good.* The Buckeye was a stable trainer. Engine response was quick. He had ninety degrees of turn to go before rolling out straight and level, hopefully lined up with the ship's small, angled runway.

What the heck? From his left field of vision, there was an almost blinding light that seemed to be coming from his left wingtip. Scanning his instruments, Quintin struggled to take a closer look, but a quick glance at the source of the light was all he dared to spare. *Focus on what's ahead, damn it*, he thought. With about forty-five degrees to go, Quintin could pick up the Fresnel lens, also called the meatball. The device, named after its French inventor, was used to gauge a pilot's position in the sky relative to the ship just before landing. If the plane was on glide path, the center light lined up with the horizontal green datum lights. The light turned brighter white if above the glide path and darker red if below the glide path. "Red you're dead" meant a likely ramp strike and almost certain death. If the pilots or crew ejected just before hitting the back end of the ship, they would hopefully survive. However, the ensuing crash, fireball, and explosion would cause major destruction to the ship and almost certain loss of life to flight deck personnel. That would not look good for career advancement!

That light off to the side—what the heck is that? It was just outside his direct visual field but close enough for him to see it and feel it. It was still with him. *There's movement in the light. Oh crap! Am I on fire?* As the Buckeye rolled wings level, Quintin's aircraft's position looked okay; the meatball was near center, lineup was good, and descent and airspeed were acceptable.

"Nine seven nine, call the ball," radioed the landing signal officer (LSO), letting each pilot know he had to respond. A response quickly identified one's aircraft number and confirmed sighting of the meatball, the fuel state in thousands of pounds, and the pilot's last name. However, the LSOs often heard only garbled words that were incomprehensible. The LSOs, having been there before, understood the anxiety and the current state of mind of each student. The aircraft's position in the sky, attitude, speed, and approach to the back end of the carrier were all the communication they needed. "Add power" or lineup adjustments were often called. "Wave off" was the order given to abandon the landing attempt due to being outside the window of a safe landing. Any instructions radioed by the LSOs to the students were to be obeyed without question or hesitation. The discipline indoctrinated in them in AOCS and flight school paid off in moments like those.

The scan went from mostly inside instruments to outside: lineup, attitude of nose, descent, and small corrections on the stick and throttles. Quintin called the ball, and the LSOs responded with a seemingly relaxed response: "Roger ball." In essence, that was their reply to the pilot to show that everyone was on the same page and that a successful landing was anticipated. Less than twenty seconds later, the aircraft touched—or slammed—onto the steel deck.

The T-2 Buckeye hit the flight deck quicker than Quintin had thought it would, and it caught him somewhat by surprise. At a descent rate of approximately eighteen feet per second, Quintin expected a cushioned touchdown, but it was not even close. The hard seat the pilot sat on was not prone to comfort, especially for a pilot with little natural cushion. The small checklist clipped to the board wrapped around his right thigh slid down his leg, and the jolt on his spine forced a gasp, almost knocking the wind out of him. Quintin jammed the throttles to full power with his left hand and slightly pulled back on the stick. He was airborne once again almost instantly.

That wasn't too bad, he thought. A couple hundred feet of runway ended quickly when one was going one hundred miles per hour. Without enough airspeed, the wings had no lift, and with no lift, the pilot faced surviving a ditch at sea. There were stories of guys hitting the water, surviving the impact, and successfully exiting the aircraft only to get sucked underneath by the ship's massive propellers. Other stories told of pilots ejected and slammed against the ship's superstructure or multitude of antennae on their way out from the doomed aircraft. Some ejections were initially successful only to slam down on one of the many hard objects on the flight deck before the parachute had time to fully open.

Once safely airborne, Quintin was able to take some inventory and process the overload of visual stimuli. He took another look at the left wingtip. Nothing. No lights, no movement, and no fire. *What the heck?* he thought. He climbed to the landing pattern at six hundred feet and looked upwind to make sure no one was coming on downwind. As he completed the second touch-and-go, he realized the light had not returned. *No time to think about that now. If it was a fire, it's no longer there. Focus, damn it!*

On the third pass, the hook came down. It was time

now for the first arrested landing. The navy required two hookup landings, or touch-and-gos, and four arrested landings to qualify. On downwind, he quickly completed the ten-item landing checklist as he readied for another pass. As with the previous two touch-and-gos, he got to a decent start and called the ball. When he felt the aircraft hit the deck, as before, he added full power. This time, one of the four steel cables on the ship's deck was caught by the hook. He felt a wicked deceleration as he was forcibly lunged forward and face-planted right on the instrument panel. Quintin hit so hard that he was dazed and felt a warm flow over his mouth. His upper lip and nose felt as if he had just been struck with a bat, and his mouth filled with blood from biting his tongue. If not for his helmet, visor, and oxygen mask, the outcome would've been uglier. The Buckeye was now on the deck in full power, held in place by the still-attached steel cable.

"Nine seven nine, throttle back, son. We got ya," radioed the air boss.

"Yes, sir." Quintin's response was garbled.

As he throttled back to idle, the cable released him, and he was signaled to follow the taxi director—or yellow shirt, as taxi directors were called—on the flight deck. He looked at Quintin and shook his head. As Quintin followed the yellow shirt's taxi instructions, he thought, *This guy, the air boss, and the whole ship must think I'm a dumbass.* " After the taxi director gave Quintin the signal to stop so they could chain him down, the yellow shirt then put his right fist into the palm of his left hand and quickly removed it—the symbolic gesture for "Get your head out of your ass!"

Yep, that's exactly what they think of me, he concluded. Quintin gave him the middle finger in his mind.

They chained the aircraft to the deck and proceeded to refuel his trusty flying steed. During those few minutes, he was able to observe the microworld outside the cockpit: the carrier flight deck. It was a reality check. He'd done it! "On the deck of *Lady Lex*! Yeehaw!" he screamed into his bloodied mask, making sure he was not transmitting on the radio.

The flight deck was a busy place. Several other students' aircraft were chained beside him. As they listened to the communications, he heard that one of his classmates was about to land hook down. As the pilot called the ball, Quintin could not understand anything he said. "Roger ball" came back from the LSO in a slow, frustrated tone. "Right for lineup. A little power," the LSO radioed. The student responded to the instructions from the LSO. Quintin could see his classmate land and catch a wire. It didn't look as if he was face-planted. *That was reserved just for me*, he thought. "You live and die by the checklist," he muttered. He had gone through the ten items on the landing checklist but had forgotten one: to lock his harness. Fortunately, it had not been too costly a mistake. It was one he would never make again.

Once refueled and unchained, he taxied to the catapult for takeoff. He needed to successfully complete three more safe arrested landings to qualify. Slowly maneuvering the Buckeye into the takeoff position, he could hear and occasionally feel a clunk or two under the nose of the aircraft. The deck personnel were busy attaching his aircraft's nose gear to the steam catapult. When the aircraft shooter gave the sign to power up, Quintin advanced both throttles to full power, completed his takeoff checklist, and was ready to slingshot off the carrier. He scanned his instruments for any abnormality and checked his flight controls. All seemed good to go as he completed his takeoff checks. He looked at the shooter and saluted him, signaling, "I'm ready to go flying." Quintin was ready to get slung off the bow of the ship. The shooter checked for a clear runway and then bent down and touched the flight deck, giving the universal signal that an aircraft was about to launch.

The Buckeye was shaking in full power, when suddenly, there was a hard clunk, and Quintin felt an acceleration like nothing he had ever experienced before. After partially blacking out, he woke up airborne after being slung off the bow. As he recaged his brain, he thought, *That was painful. Zero to a hundred forty miles per hour in less than three seconds. No carnival ride ever prepared me for that.*

After the four arrested landings, the LSO radioed, "Nine seven nine, you're a qual," signifying Quintin had successfully qualified landing aboard an aircraft carrier.

"Thank you, sir," Quintin radioed back.

On the flight back to Boca Chica Naval Air Station, one of his classmates was told to join on his wing as the two birds made their way back to base. Upon landing, their excitement turned to jubilation.

"Dude! We qualified!"

They had joined an elite club, and they knew it. Though there were still challenges to face that would prove to be more difficult, such as flying at night and performing bad-weather landings on carriers, they'd taken a major step that day toward the coveted wings of gold on the road to becoming naval aviators.

Unfortunately, sometime later, fate left its mark. A student pilot wasn't as lucky on his final approach aboard *Lady Lex*. On final approach to landing on the ship, he was underpowered and too slow. The LSOs yelled for power repeatedly; unfortunately, the student was not quick enough in applying full throttle. The Buckeye stalled only a few feet from the rear of the ship and rolled 160 degrees to almost completely inverted as deck personnel ran for their lives. It slammed onto the back end of the flight deck, killing the student instantly, and the ensuing fireball, traveling at more than eighty miles per hour, now a heap of mangled, burning metal, quickly spread onto nearby chained-down aircraft and ground crew. Several young seamen standing on the flight deck were killed, and the ship sustained extensive damage. Naval aviation was extremely hazardous.

On that day, however, the young pilots, who had been AOCS poopies just eighteen months prior, were now the newest tail hookers. There would be celebrations that night in Key West. The world was just not big enough that night.

CHAPTER 9

Hialeah, 1975

"Coqui, *no salgas afuera con el pelo mojado*! *Te va dar una neumonía*!" Yelled Quintin's mother.

Quintin's family nickname, Coqui, had been given to him by his uncle Luis Jr. when he was born. "That boy is so white he looks like the inside of a coconut," Luis Jr. had said. The nickname had stuck, much to the chagrin of the now twelve-year-old boy.

Since leaving Cuba, Milva has had a heavy heart. She'd followed her husband to a new country to give their children a better life. The loss of her father just two years after their departure from Cuba in November 1968 had left a deep wound. She had peace in knowing her older brother was looking after their mother, Aunt Liche, and their special-needs younger brother, Oswald, or Ozzie, as he was affectionately known. Luis Jr. had a wife and two kids of his own, as well as his medical practice in their hometown in Cuba. It fell on him to help their parents and special-needs brother. However, Milva's mother's health was worsening. Luis Jr. had sent word that their mother had been suffering from memory loss and irrational behavioral outbursts in recent months. He was also frustrated at the increasing lack of medications to treat her and his patients.

In mid-December 1974, Micaela suffered a severe stroke. Despite Luis Jr.'s and his colleagues' best efforts, she passed away two days later. Two weeks after that, Luis Jr. was in his home one late afternoon, when he apparently collapsed, and he died later that evening. The news trickled in slowly via telephone calls to Miami. Several family members had gotten word and immediately came over to Ciso and Milva's house in Hialeah, expecting the worst. As more phone calls and details came in, Milva was told Luis Jr. had been suffering from insomnia for some time and had fallen into a state of depression. As he'd tried to calm his worsening anxiety and depression, he'd overmedicated himself with sedatives, which had stopped his breathing. Some believed his death was accidental; others suspected it was not. No one knew exactly what had happened, including his wife.

Milva had always been close to him, and the news was devastating. Losing her mother two weeks earlier and now her older brother took a heavy toll on her. She didn't have much choice but to muster all the strength she had for her own family as well as the family she had left on the island. Adding to her mourning was concern as to who would or could care for her younger brother, Ozzie, who required constant care. Surviving relatives or trusted friends to care for him were hard to come by.

Twelve-year-old Quintin and his sister realized that Christmas 1974 was the worst holiday for their family since their arrival in the United States six years earlier. Quintin didn't fully grasp the depth of the situation, but he hated seeing his mother with such deep sadness for so many weeks.

The Cuban revolution had been divisive for many families. Most supporters of the new government had fled the island for the United States when they realized they had supported a tyrant. Milva made those exiled groups a target of her disdain. Her parents, advanced in years, had made the fateful decision to stay in Cuba to support their oldest son's family while caring for their youngest, Ozzie, knowing what the regime was bringing. The Cuban exiles in South Florida were a taboo subject in Milva's presence.

"The majority of the exiled community in South Florida helped place that SOB in power," she often said with anger and disdain. The only common bond between the exiled community and Milva was their mutual hatred of the Cuban Communist party. "The exiles left the island and supported the US embargo on Cuba, which only hurt the island residents, while they filled their bellies in the States, and my family got stuck! *Que se vayan todos par carajo!*" she routinely muttered.

"Milva, sending the entire exiled community to hell is not going to solve anything except make you bitter!"

Ciso would say, trying to console her, which only made matters worse.

"I lost my family despite them warning everyone of the coming disaster. You, your family, and a lot of exiled Cubans here in the United States didn't listen. If you would've, we wouldn't be in this predicament." Milva often blamed Ciso and his family for not listening to her family's warnings.

Quintin and his sister witnessed the tension between their parents on the subject time and again. It was an open wound that forever was exposed, and it became woven in the fabric of their marriage for years.

With the extensive urban expansion in Hialeah, farmland was quickly shrinking. Many of the tracts of land were converted to high-rise, high-density occupancy to house the constant arrival of immigrants. The population was growing rapidly, as well as the area's economics. With such rapid and poorly controlled urban planning, however, congestion, incivility, and crime were on the rise. Quintin witnessed the disappearance of the former mango grove that he and his childhood buddies had run through and enjoyed climbing just a few short years earlier. Still, Ciso, Milva, and their two young kids were free and living a life they had only dreamed of in Cuba.

"You are such a mama's boy!" barked his sister, Margret. "Going outside with wet hair has nothing to do with getting sick. You're just too stupid to realize it!"

Quintin had always been close to his mother. Reluctantly, he knew he was a mama's boy. Still, getting openly chastised by his older sister was not going to go unchallenged, even though in his heart, there was no winning this one.

"Margret, leave the boy alone," snapped his father.

Ciso had found work as a backhoe operator in construction and had plenty of work when the construction industry was good. The family had moved from Los Angeles, California, to Hialeah in 1971 for better employment opportunities. He enjoyed working outside, despite the heat and humidity of Florida, especially during the summer months. Quintin accompanied him on many work projects. Even at twelve years of age, he got to know the business of heavy construction. To the dismay of his father, it was not what Quintin wanted as a profession. His dreams and aspirations were different from his father's practical dreams.

"*Tu sabes*, Coqui, *construcción es un buen trabajo*."

"Dad, I don't like construction. I want to fly jets."

"*O cara*. Yes, I know you do, but be realistic, *hijo*. As you get older, we can work together. I'll show you the business. Besides, you'll never fly jets for the navy. That's a wild goose chase. The military is not for you! They tell you what to wear, how to behave, and what you can and cannot do. They own you. That's no way to live!" Ciso often reinforced what he thought was best for his son.

Despite the lack of encouragement, Quintin's desire to fly supersonic jets, engage in classic dogfights like the heroes he read about, and live for adventure was a dream he could not squelch. At twelve, Quintin hoped to take flying lessons; however, the family's finances would not allow it. Besides, as he later found out, he was too young anyway.

Ciso would have none of it. "Too dangerous. Forget it. *Nunca!*"

Quintin resigned himself to reading whatever he could about flying. He read magazines like *Air and Space*, *Modern Fighters*, and *Jane's Military Aircraft* and absorbed them in detail. His bedroom was covered in military posters of navy pilots, astronauts, and aircraft. He built models and went to every airshow within a couple of hours from their home. One such show was at Homestead Air Force Base. Quintin was able to see an F-4 Phantom from the Air National Guard. The aircrew were giving the public a personal tour of the jet. People made their way up the short ladder and took turns sitting in the pilot's office, as he called it. Quintin was speechless when it was his turn to sit in the pilot's seat. At twelve years of age, his eyes lusted at the cockpit controls and flight stick.

"Well, how do you like sitting in the F-4, young man?" asked the pilot. Quintin was so excited that he only smiled without looking up at him. "I can see you're quite impressed. Maybe you can join us in a few years. Keep working hard, and stay out of trouble!"

Quintin stepped out of the cockpit and thanked him. Ciso watched him climb down, noticed a grin from ear to ear on his son's face, and said, "*O cara.*" Quintin knew at that moment without any doubt he had confirmed his life's passion.

"Why can't I go outside with my hair wet after eating, Mom? Margret says it's not true that I'll get sick."

"I told you. You can get pneumonia or an embolism. It happened to my cousin Ivette," responded Milva.

"Mom, how do you catch pneumonia if your hair is wet?" asked her confused and frustrated son.

"Trust me. I know. Now, do as I say, hmm?" His mother gave him a stern look and again stressed the importance of drying his hair.

Quintin knew there was no winning an argument with his mother when it came to passed-down old wives' tales, especially those regarding her children's safety. For example, her insistence on a spoonful of daily cod liver oil, Mercurochrome for any skin cuts, and Vicks VapoRub spread on the chest before bed when he was fighting an upper respiratory infection was nonnegotiable.

Thirty minutes later, with dry hair, Quintin ran outside to play manhunt with his friends.

"You're coddling that boy too much, woman! He's

gonna grow up to be a sissy." Ciso would not tolerate any gestures or treatment of his son he considered feminine.

"I don't care," responded Milva. "He'll be fine. I recently read that General Douglas MacArthur was a mama's boy, and look how he turned out."

Ciso always insisted that his son demonstrate masculine attributes. On one occasion, when Quintin was twelve years old, his father scolded him for blow-drying his hair. "*Eso es para mujeres*," Ciso told him, drawing a silly conclusion that only women blow-dried their hair.

Ironically, several years later, when Quintin was in high school, he caught Ciso drying his own hair with a blow dryer. Not able to pass on the golden opportunity to tease him, he said, "Dad, you're turning into a woman at your age? Tell me it isn't so!" His father ignored him. It took Quintin several minutes before he finally stopped laughing at his old man.

Their home was a three-bedroom, two-bath home. It was simple yet comfortable, with a red shag carpet, used appliances, and used furniture. Ciso was content, and he and Milva settled down to make a life for themselves in that little corner of northwest Dade County, Florida. Quintin and his family met the original owners during the home showing in the summer of 1972. The lady of the house showed his family their modest ranch-style home and settled in the living room to answer any questions they had about the house. On one wall, there were pictures of one of her sons, who had served in the Vietnam War. She didn't smile, and it seemed to Quintin she was sad. He didn't fully understand the moment, but the look on Quintin's mother's face reflected pain and sorrow that he would never forget. The woman's son, only eighteen years old, had been killed in action several months earlier. The lady of the house had trouble speaking about him, and to Quintin, she seemed to be out of breath.

Upon hearing of the tragedy, Milva grew pale, and Ciso quietly said, "*O cara*," as he turned his gaze to the floor.

For almost an hour after they left, Milva wiped tears from her face. "That poor mother," she repeated over and over.

Once they had settled into their new home, they quickly found out there were plenty of neighborhood kids. They were not shy in getting to know one another, and that usually happened through street football, baseball, or hide-and-seek. Quintin and Margret made many friends, and some lasted a lifetime. Every afternoon, upon arriving home from school, Quintin couldn't wait to run through someone's yard, go swimming in someone else's pool, climb trees, build tree houses, and participate in many other outdoor activities with his friends well into the night.

"*Hola*," said a loud voice from outside their carport door as they heard a loud knock. "*Buenos dias.* Good day."

As Margret opened the door, she recognized Lipio

standing there with a wide grin, showing off his large white teeth. "Hi, Lipio," she said as she greeted him with a hug.

Lipio had arrived in the United States three years prior and was working construction as a backhoe operator. He was learning to speak English and constantly practiced it with anyone who would put up with and listen to his constant verbal translation. "Hello, little girl Margret. That means '*Hola, niña* Margret.'"

"Yes, I know," responded Margret, rolling her eyes. She and her brother, Quintin, had learned English easily, and, like most immigrant kids, had become fluent within just six months after arriving in the States. It took their parents and Lipio a little more time to become fluent, but they did.

"*Hola*, Lipio. *Que pasa*? How's the construction business?" asked Ciso.

"Same. Up and down, you know." Miami in the early to mid-1970s was experiencing a construction boom, and both men were busy and hungry for more. "I was digging a trench for a building foundation in downtown, when *fuacata*! I blew a hydraulic line. The brakes need replacing as well. But that old Ford 5500 gets the job done."

"*Si*, there are plenty of parts too," replied Ciso. He then added, "There's nothing like the free market of capitalism—supply and demand. It sure beats the stagnant inefficiency of those *comunistas, que come-mierda son*!"

"*Absolutamente*! *Los Yankees son bien inteligente*," replied Lipio.

Lipio was a frequent visitor at their home. One day Lipio privately revealed to Ciso he had received a call from Cuba regarding a woman he knew and had courted after being released from the work camp. She had been able to visit Honduras on a state-sponsored visit, and he had flown out to meet her there fourteen months ago. After several days together, she'd returned to the island with plans that Lipio would sponsor her if she were to seek asylum in the States. As time marched on, as far as he knew, she had been unsuccessful in obtaining an exit visa. The months had passed, and communication between the two of them had ceased.

"One week ago, I received a letter from her sister saying she had met an intelligence official and married him some time ago. I'm not sure if she was already with this man when she flew to Honduras to meet me," Lipio said. "In either case, the letter went further. There's a six-month-old boy, and she claims I'm the father!"

"Well, are you?" asked Ciso.

"*No estoy seguro*!" responded Lipio.

"You don't know? You think maybe the official's the father? What are you going to do, amigo?"

Lipio's usual grin was nowhere to be found. His eyes stared about the room. "If that's my kid, I'm gonna try to get him to come here."

"You think she's just going to let her son go and come here with you, apart from her? Don't be an *idiota*," responded Ciso.

"It's not just that. The letter says the husband doesn't want the child. Apparently, he doesn't believe the child is his, and he's threatening to place the child up for adoption as a ward of the state."

"*O cara. ¡No creo eso!*" responded Ciso.

The two of them sat quietly on the back porch, pondering Lipio's predicament.

"*Hola*, Lipio." Milva greeted him upon entering the room to say hello.

"*Hola, señora maestra.* How is your day?" responded Lipio, practicing English with his heavy Spanish accent.

"You're getting better and better," she replied while ignoring her husband. Lipio smiled from ear to ear at her approval of his new and ever-improving language skills.

In the years that followed, the tension between Ciso and Milva grew increasingly higher and was felt in their home. Quintin's parents argued more frequently, and he and his sister were not blind to it.

One week, Milva asked her husband repeatedly for new living room furniture since theirs consisted of hand-me-downs from a friend and was now in disrepair. Tired of hearing her complain, he finally consented and agreed she should order new furniture and stop pestering him. After she chose a set, it was delivered to their home and set up by delivery personnel. Later that afternoon, Ciso arrived, saw the furniture, and called the delivery driver to come back to pick up the furniture. He accused her of trying to dominate him and take away his authority by not including him in the decision to choose and purchase the furniture. He believed he should have been the final word on any purchase. His machismo was alive and well and on full display, which made her feel hurt and dismayed. Milva stood by silently while they carried the furniture away and put the old set back in its place. She was an obedient wife and often relented even when she knew her husband was in the wrong.

"It is always easier to let him have his way than to create strife," she would say to justify her behavior to herself and others.

No matter the state of their relationship, divorce was unthinkable. There was a stigma about divorce for her generation. She never wanted to be the subject of gossip or scorn. "I feel sorry for him," she often said. "If I leave him, he'll have no one to take care of him. He'll be all alone." For years, she dealt with his chauvinism silently while fulfilling her role as a wife and mother as best as she could.

CHAPTER 10

In the Smokies II

"Wow! I love that smell," said Quintin as he watched his wife bring him a bowl of red beans with smoked ham on a bed of white rice. She always prepared oven turkey and other accompanying dishes days before their camping trip in order to maximize their outdoor time. The rich aroma filled the evening air around the campfire. "The only thing missing is fried plantains and flan."

"Excuse me? *Que te pasa?*" she snapped. "I have homemade flan, and the plantains are from the supermarket, pre fried and frozen. Not as good as the real thing but close enough."

"For sure, baby girl."

Their culinary skills had greatly improved over time, mostly due to necessity while living in small-town Tennessee, since their only options were, for the most part, fast food restaurants. The scarce dining options had forced their cooking education.

"Your mother and your grandmother would be proud of how far we've come in reproducing our traditional Cuban dishes. Even though I have to admit, you've always hated cooking," Quintin said. "It's funny when I think of Mimi's friend's first experience with plantains several months ago. I offered a cut-up fried plantain to her, and she picked it up, stared at it, and, after asking what it was, sort of gagged but proceeded to put it in her mouth anyway. Almost instantly, she spit it out and said, 'That's gross!'"

They both chuckled.

"You know, some of the locals have never even left the county," Quintin added. "It's strange to think about that. It's a different world up here compared to South Florida. Take our neighbor who came over earlier, for example. It seems to me he embodies the current Appalachian people: simple and honest in their ways yet ignorant to the ways of the world beyond these mountains, almost innocent. I wonder if the original Indian natives were not much different in their interactions with the Europeans." He paused. "I must be boring you. It's just that I think of them often—I mean the original natives."

Cari smiled.

Quintin continued. "They were a completely different culture with a completely different way of life, yet in the end, I believe we all want the same things out of life. Besides, the native peoples were free. Free to make their own choices and walk into the future without any guarantees. Without freedom, someone else is deciding life and how you are to live it. That's not something I ever want.

"Freedom! To live life to the fullest while you can

and how you see fit—that's what it's all about. Yes, I know you always remind me it has to be done responsibly. Imagine—each day they lived must've been as if it was going to be their last."

Quintin paused for a moment. "Ciso lived to be free. It was not just important to him but vital, like air and water. I believe that way too. Much has been written regarding the cost of liberty. Good grief, imagine life without it. My father got a taste of it in Cuba, and he said he would rather die than return to that soul-crushing system. What do you think?"

Before Cari could answer, Quintin continued. "That being said, from what little I know of that time period, the encounter with the Spanish cost the Indians their all. Yep, it's sad when you really think about it. I'm not a sociologist, but I wonder if progress, or the lack thereof, is what ultimately sealed their fate. Or was it a combination of factors? Heck, I don't know. I just can't stop thinking about them when we are out here. Someday I hope our kids, nephews, and niece really understand the sacrifices of their grandparents. I'm sure they will in time. Because one thing's for sure: at their current age, they can't see beyond their noses. Neither did we, right? You look so beautiful in the light of the fire."

Cari's smile brightened. She placed her fingers to her lips and blew him a kiss.

"Good evening, neighbor and fellow camper."

"Good evening to you," responded Quintin as he watched a couple stroll by, walking their dog.

Quintin and Cari's two kids, now older, were too busy with their respective social lives to join them in camping these days. Their son, Joe, was twenty-one and was trying his hand at real estate. Although he had turned his back on what his parents felt were his true talents, such as violin, piano, and the gift of articulation, he was working hard toward his dreams. Quintin often said they would have to accept that journalism, music, and maybe even law school were the dreams they had for him and not his own. He was determined and working on his career. He always hoped for fast money.

"Fast money? What a bunch of bologna! There's no such thing," Quintin often told his son.

"Yes, Dad, there is. You want to work smarter, not harder, remember?"

Quintin was concerned about his son's outlook and work ethic going forward. "Sometimes I feel like I failed as a father," he told Cari. He thought Joe's lifestyle gave him unrealistic expectations and unhealthy goals.

"He'll grow up. Give him time," his wife often reminded him. Sometimes she would say it without Quintin saying a word, almost as if she knew what he was thinking. After thirty years of marriage, being unpredictable was not one of his character traits.

Their daughter, Michaela, or Mimi, as she was fondly

called, was currently a junior in high school and known for her large-and-in-charge attitude. She was an opinionated, witty, street-smart girl with an attitude to match. She, like many her age, relied heavily on her smartphone, as if it were an electronic lifeline.

He and his wife did a good job, he thought. Even if their kids choose different paths than Quintin and Cari imagined, they were going to be okay.

While they dined under the stars that peeked through the tree canopy, the nearby majestic trees seemed to move with the light of the campfire. The fire was warm and welcoming. *No need for another log*, he thought. Quintin turned his gaze and listened to his wife as she spoke, only partially paying attention. His thoughts often wandered during their conversations. It was a trait that served him well with long-winded individuals and caused him some embarrassment when questioned. He had learned to focus better with his wife to avoid her rebuke for his lack of attention. This time, she was the cause of his distraction. He was admiring her beautiful, long dark hair; sharp lips; curvy lines; and other beautiful features. He was truly and totally in love with this creature.

After he cleaned up and put things away, he recalled when they first met. Thoughts of that warm summer night in June thirty-five years earlier came rushing back.

CHAPTER 11

At the Pool, Summer 1985

Just another warm summer night at the city pool, thought Quintin as he settled into the tall lifeguard chair. There were dozens of kids playing. Many of them splashed in a frenzy as they cooled off in the late afternoon. Some were obviously comfortable in showing off their skills, while others were not. *Not sure which is more dangerous*, he thought.

Looking across the pool at his fellow guard, he noticed a young girl below the lifeguard chair. She had long, straight dark hair that flowed like silk into the water. He felt there was something different about her, even though he could only see her from behind. Quintin found it difficult to draw his attention elsewhere. He forced his gaze to other swimmers, but irresistible curiosity forced him back. *Stop staring*, he thought.

It was too late—one of the other two girls with her saw him staring at them, and almost as if on cue, they appeared to synchronize their movements as all three turned to look at him. Finally, he got to see her face. "Oh no," he whispered to himself. She smiled at him, said something quick to the others, and swam over.

Quintin was inexplicably nervous. He had been

wondering for some time now what kind of girl he might marry one day. He had a general idea of someone who was kind and family oriented and, most importantly, had a relationship with God. He couldn't really explain why God was so important. He only knew that as a believer, he felt that finding a fellow believer would somehow align life's priorities. Currently, his spiritual life wasn't as strong as it should have been; still, it was important to him that his future wife was a strong Christian. His faith was a subject weighing on his heart. He still wrestled with questions such as "Who is God?" and "If he exists, why does he feel so distant?" Growing up Catholic, Quintin never had been truly immersed in religion, much less faith. He and his family did the usual Catholic mass on Easter and occasionally attended church on Christmas, but that was about it. When he was a young boy, his mother often prayed with him before bed and recited the Lord's Prayer. She had done it so often he had committed the prayer to memory in Spanish. Over the past few years, Quintin had felt a growing hole or void in his heart that kept him pondering purpose, the meaning of life, and the future, including the person he would eventually want to spend the rest of his life with. He was twenty-two, and the social escapades of hanging with his buddies were getting old and felt unfulfilling. He was a year away from graduating from college and going after his childhood dream of flying adventures in the US Navy.

Her pretty smile was hard to miss. She had straight, long black hair with pretty bangs and perfectly straight white teeth. "Hi," she said when she and her friends boldly approached him. "Were you staring at us?" she asked.

"No," he said, "not at all. Well, if I was, I didn't mean to." His heart was racing. *Why am I nervous?* he thought. *This is ridiculous.*

"I'm Cari."

Cari then introduced her sister and cousin to him. Quintin was curious and nervous at the same time. Cari appeared to Quintin to be kind, friendly, and self-confident. He, on the other hand, was anxious, clumsy, and a bit confused, and he was sure it showed. After formal introductions, small talk ensued as they slowly got to know each other.

Suddenly, with no warning, Cari unexpectedly grabbed the skin on the right side of her neck and wiggled it. "I have a shunt. It was implanted in me when I was a baby due to my hydrocephalus."

"Hydro what?" he said with his mouth wide open.

"I was born with too much water in my brain and had to have it shunted into my abdomen."

"Okay." It was the only word he was able to come up with. He tried desperately to conceal his speechless, wide-eyed demeanor and even harder not to stare at her neck, but he failed miserably.

"I figured it would come up in our conversation sooner or later, so there it is."

After a moment, he was able to compose himself. "My name is Quintin."

"Yes, I know," she said. The rest of the conversation Quintin would never remember.

That night, as he drove home in his VW Bug, he thought there was something definitely different about Cari. She had a certain maturity and depth to her that he had never before seen, and he felt things he never had felt with anyone else. Yet there was something else. He didn't yet realize it, but Cari had inexplicably filled a hole in Quintin's heart, as if the last piece of a thousand-piece jigsaw puzzle was now in place and complete. *She's gotta be at least seventeen*, he thought. *Is she the one?* He couldn't explain it, but he had a sense of peace about her. *Yes*, he concluded, *she must be the one!*

"Wait, no, no way. What am I doing? Settle down, dude," he told himself aloud. He was confused, and for the rest of the night, he couldn't stop thinking about her. At twenty-two, he had dated other girls before. *Girls are beautiful, but girls can be such bitches. But this one is different. At least she seems to be.*

Quintin was experiencing something entirely different. He was in uncharted waters. Deep emotions with flashes of future relational permanence were taking root within him. Periodically, reality would remind him of the present. His dream of a career in aviation had been, up to that point, his true love, and his usual mantra of "No distractions and no commitments" was nonnegotiable. With this unexpected encounter, however, it was as if lightning had struck him. For the first time in Quintin's life, the solid rock foundation of his love of flying, with room for no one else, had a serious crack.

Later that night, as he lay in his bed, Quintin stared at the ceiling, wondering about the future. His plan of joining the navy after graduating from college was paramount. "Only twelve more months, and I'm done with campus life. I can't let anything or anyone derail me from my dream. Still, I hope she comes back to the pool." It took him a while to fall asleep that evening. Somehow, he knew deep inside that something had changed forever.

The summer of 1985 was off to a great start. Quintin was content to have a job as a lifeguard, especially at $4.50 an hour. It was great pay to stand or, even better, sit and watch people enjoy themselves in the pool while he worked on his tan. The other lifeguards were college students as well, except one. Jimmy was the only other male on the team of five. He had recently left school, as he was contemplating other pursuits. His curly blond hair and muscular tan body made him a favorite of many young girls. He was friendly, unassuming, and mellow. The head lifeguard, Joann, was concerned about him and confronted him on several occasions for being late.

One afternoon, as Jimmy came in to work, Quintin overheard their exchange before they opened the pool to the public. Joann asked, "Which Jimmy is showing up today?"

Jimmy responded, "What the hell do you mean?"

Joann responded, "You and I both know what I mean. Look at you. Your eyes are red. What are you on?"

"Nah, man, I'm good. Relax."

"Don't tell me to relax, you dumbass! Go home, get some sleep, and don't show up again stoned or whatever you're on. Time after time, you show up late without much argument from me. Get this: we all depend on one another here, not to mention that these kids deserve better. If you do this again, I'll be speaking with the Department of Recreations at city management."

Joann took her job as lead lifeguard seriously. Her demeanor and strength sent a clear message, one that Jimmy would not dare to cross. He silently walked back to his car and drove away.

"Are you okay?" asked Quintin.

"Yeah," Joann responded. "It burns me up when someone is not reliable. Besides, I caught him and one of his girlfriends all over each other several nights ago here in the office!"

Quintin's eyes widened. "You mean Cathy?"

"No, not Cathy. The girl he was with is a lifeguard I

recognized from training. She works at the south pool, not here."

Quintin was relieved it wasn't anyone from their team. He had a newfound respect for Joann's leadership and her resolve to do what was right. *She's a natural leader*, he thought.

It wasn't long before his new friend Cari and her relatives returned to the pool. When he saw her, he was filled with sweet thoughts of how much of an impact she had unintentionally made on him. *How can this be?* he thought. *I just met her.*

Once they started talking again, he was rocked to his core when she told him she was fourteen, not seventeen, as he originally had imagined. The news hit him like a freight train. He was twenty-two and might as well have been sixty-two, for that matter. *Ugh*, he thought. *This cannot be! There is no way I am going to date her. There's no way I can, even though I want to. It's weird even thinking about it. Almost creepy.* Putting aside how it would have looked that he was eight years older, he was sure her parents and family were not going to have any of it. Hispanics tended to be extremely protective of their daughters, especially teenage girls.

Still, when he thought of her, he couldn't help the ever-deepening and growing feelings he had for her. There was a mysterious excitement in the newness of their friendship. Now, because of their age difference, there was a possibility it was an unlikely relationship. He kept those emotions to himself over the next few days, despite his best friends noticing a change in him and pestering him regarding the stupid grin on his face.

"Dude, what the heck is going on?" Both Randy and Paulo knew something had changed.

"Nothing! It's all good," Quintin responded, hoping they would drop the subject.

"You lying piece of dog turd. What's her name?" asked Randy.

Quintin tried to get them off the trail, but to no avail. He finally told them about her, only sharing her name and conveniently avoiding details, such as her age.

As the weeks passed, Cari and Quintin grew closer in friendship, and there was definite chemistry between them. They were both cautious, never allowing anyone, especially her family members, to suspect, or so they thought. Captured moments of eye contact and quick hellos were cherished. One afternoon, after the pool closed, he shared Starburst candy with her while her younger sister, cousin, and friends made sure they were never far off. They were always circling and staring, yet it didn't bother Quintin; he knew they were watching out for her and curious about their budding friendship. Besides, with teenage girls, if there was going to be any drama, they wanted a front-row seat. Cari and Quintin shared with each other their favorite Starburst flavors. It wasn't until much later that Cari informed him she never had liked Starburst. Her kindness and friendliness were matched by her confidence and wisdom, which he thought were well beyond her years.

Ultimately, secrecy did not delay its betrayal. News of their friendship slowly spread, and as expected, it was not well received. Shortly thereafter, a small inquisition was born.

Several days passed before Cari and her family returned to the pool with news of what had transpired. Marcia, her mother, suspected something unusual. She knew her oldest daughter was not inclined to swimming or diving, yet to Marcia's surprise, she asked to go to the pool on a daily basis.

"My daughter the swimmer? Hell no. Something is brewing. What's his name?" she demanded.

By then, news of their friendship was out of the bag. Drama was no stranger to teenage girls, and drama it became.

"If you think I'm going to let my fourteen-year-old daughter date a twenty-two-year-old man, you've got rocks in your brain!" yelled her mother.

Cari's stepdad, Levi, was furious and ready for war. "A twenty two-year-old college senior? Who the hell? What the hell is going on?"

Cari tried to explain that it wasn't as it seemed or as they imagined it. "He's really nice and respectful."

"Forget it! Ain't happening. Besides, if both your grandfathers find out, there'll be hell to pay, not to mention they'll blame me. Cari, men start off nice and friendly, and then, before you know it, they'll try to get in your skirt!" yelled Marcia. "Levi, get me a drink with plenty of alcohol."

"You don't drink," he said.

"Just do it!" Marcia said.

As Quintin returned to his final year at the university, he and Cari started writing to each other. They stayed close despite rarely seeing each other in the following months. In February of the following year, she, with her parents' permission, invited him to her fifteenth birthday party, a traditional and festive occasion in Hispanic culture. Her parents realized they were better off allowing them to be friends than forbidding her from seeing him at all. Quintin drove the six hours from Gainesville and, to everyone's surprise, brought along his mother, Milva. To the birthday girl and her family, the presence of Quintin and his mother broadcast something loud and clear: the slightly improper and improbable relationship of theirs was taking on a whole new twist. Most of her family were in attendance, and their reactions, although cautious, were heartfelt toward Quintin.

At least they didn't tell me to get the hell out of here! he thought. Quintin did not feel unwelcome, even with occasional blank stares.

"Who is this man? Cari is only fifteen. What is going on?" some family members asked.

"He is a friend," Cari responded.

"He doesn't look at you like a friend," said her stepdad. Levi was a caring and concerned stepfather to Cari and her sister. He had stepped in, and many in the family acknowledged that Marcia had won the lottery with such a good man who loved her and her daughters. The presence of Quintin's mother at the birthday party helped bring down the temperature in the room.

"My name is Levi. Who are you, and what do you want with my daughter?"

"I'm Quintin. We are friends. We met at the pool last summer."

After Quintin explained his honorable intentions, Levi seemed to tolerate Quintin's presence, at least for the moment. He kept a close eye on the young man hovering around his fifteen-year-old daughter. Levi was not alone in his reservations. Quintin knew tolerance did not mean acceptance.

The party was festive, with a menu of roast pork, sweet fried plantains, yucca, rice, and black beans—typical during Cuban get-togethers. The music was a mixture of Spanish salsa and contemporary pop music for 1986.

"God bless America," said one man.

A thin and short older man with a heavy Cuban accent approached Quintin. "They call me Crazy Ricky. I'm the birthday girl's best-looking uncle! Ha!" He had no verbal filter at all, and to Quintin, he seemed too comfortable with the use of profanity. Ricky wore multiple gold chains around his neck and rings on his fingers, dark blue Jordache jeans, and cheap low-cut boots. Quintin didn't know what to make of him.

"*Estas borracho!*" said one of the older women standing in a small group nearby, accusing him of being drunk.

"We can never be certain. He is always that way," said another.

"*No coman mierda,*" Ricky snapped at the ladies, whom he knew well.

"How dare you accuse us of eating crap, little man?" By then, one of the heavyset ladies had had enough of his usual nonsense, and it seemed to Quintin the situation might get testy.

"It is you people who are drunk," Ricky said with a loud chuckle.

"*Calmate*, Sira. It's better to let him make a fool of himself. Besides, we'll deal with him later."

They all seemed to agree, nodding, as if some unofficial code existed among them. They then shook their heads in disgust and proceeded to quietly ignore him.

"Ha!" blurted Ricky. He then mumbled something inaudible that Quintin felt relieved not to comprehend.

One of the young teenagers at the birthday party

approached Ricky as if to grab at his lower leg. Ricky reeled back, unsuccessfully concealing a holstered revolver strapped to his ankle. "Don't do that, my young friend," Ricky said in his heavy accent. The young teen obviously knew him well and constantly pestered him for an entertaining reaction. Ricky looked back at Quintin and once again said, "God bless America."

I'm not sure it's a good idea for this man to be carrying a weapon, let alone at a party. He's quite the character. No doubt the name Crazy Ricky is spot on, thought Quintin.

Beyond some of the cold stares from her family, Quintin knew his heart and intentions were beyond the moment. It felt right, and he knew deep down she was the One. *She's so beautiful,* he thought. Her demeanor, smile, confidence, and courage would occupy his thoughts for a long time. As before, he kept reminding himself of their age difference. *Good grief,* he thought. *If I blow it, I will face angry dads, crazy uncles, her mom, and grandparents, not to mention law enforcement, who would not hesitate to come after me with all they've got.*

Still, he thought, Cari was worth it, and he would risk his heart despite the overwhelming odds against their improbable relationship.

The following day, he headed back to Gainesville to finish his final semester at the university.

CHAPTER 12

Graduation's Beginning, 1986

The spring of 1986 brought change and the promise of adventure for Quintin. He was finally graduating from the University of Florida. "No more campus life. Time to conquer the world!" he told his college buddies. May was all about celebrating graduation with his friends before starting on his new journey. Through it all, Quintin anticipated getting home to see his parents. They had financially supported him throughout his studies, and Quintin wanted to share the momentous occasion with them.

His mother had graduated from college in Cuba and then again in the United States with a second bachelor's in education. She worked as a teacher at an elementary school near their home in Hialeah, Florida. Ciso had worked in heavy construction since arriving from California shortly after immigrating to the United States. Quintin and his sister greatly respected their parents' work ethic.

"I will never receive welfare or any financial assistance from any government," Ciso often declared proudly. Their experiences in Cuba had molded within him an iron will and a belief that reliance on any institution for basic necessities was an attempt by the institution at control and was the first step in institutional dependence.

Milva, meanwhile, was more pragmatic. With two small children, she was the homemaker, trying to feed her family and meet the day-to-day demands, while Ciso worked long hours. "If they're offering help, why not take it?" she would say.

Ciso would have none of it. "It is not someone else's responsibility to provide for this family. That is strictly my responsibility."

Milva, as usual, went along with her husband's decision, even if she disagreed.

After arriving from Cuba, the family spent the winter of 1968 and the following three years in Los Angeles, California. Ciso had worked as a welder at the Long Beach Naval Shipyard and often pulled overtime for extra income, sometimes working eighteen hours on a shift. One of his supervisors had been impressed with him, but after Ciso had told him he was from Cuba, his supervisor had scowled and let out a groan of disapproval. He'd said it was because of "those damn Cubans" that he'd had to leave South Florida. "You people will work for nothing!" he'd exclaimed.

The only response Ciso had been able to muster was "*O cara.*"

After the graduation ceremonies in Gainesville, Quintin's drive back to South Florida was exciting. The smell of orange blossoms filled the air along Florida's US-27 highway. Down the spine of Florida, many small communities were sprinkled, separated by vast acres of orange groves. *I hope my Bug makes it*, Quintin thought. His father had bought him a 1972 Volkswagen Beetle when he graduated from high school, and Quintin used it on many trips. Its air-cooled rear engine hummed as the warm air entered through the windows. Quintin's dog, Rocket, alternated between the backseat and the passenger seat; he was always stressed out on car rides. Quintin had picked him up two years earlier from a Gainesville breeder. He always had wanted a beagle, and although Rocket was the runt of the litter, he was a loyal companion and friend.

Several weeks earlier, he had adopted a tricolored beagle puppy just eight weeks old. "He's so beautiful." Quintin fell in love with his new little buddy. "I'll call you Puppy Dog till we have a good name for you." He kept him in the bathroom while he went to class and often returned to check up on him throughout the day. "I can't wait till you meet Cari and my family. They are going to love you, especially Margret. You and I are gonna have some adventures together. Oh yeah!"

As the days passed, Quintin noticed Puppy Dog was slowing down, appeared fatigued, and wasn't as playful. He decided to wait twenty-four hours and check up on him in the morning. The following day, Quintin awoke early and noticed his little buddy was worse. He called the vet's office, but it was closed on Saturdays. The nearest animal hospital was several miles away. However, the cost for a visit was too prohibitive for his college budget, which was essentially poverty. He decided to try to nurse the puppy with fluids and watch him for one more day.

"He doesn't look good, bro," Quintin's roommate, Robert, said as he noticed the pup. "I'm gonna be at my girlfriend's all weekend. See ya later."

Quintin stayed with his little buddy all day, and occasionally, the little pup would take a few gulps of water, giving Quintin encouragement. Later that night, he placed a warm blanket on the bathroom floor and placed the pup on it. He went to bed feeling better but set his alarm for early the next morning. When he awoke, he came into the bathroom and noticed Puppy Dog appeared much weaker and barely opened his eyes. Even worse, the pup vomited, which was followed shortly by bloody diarrhea.

With his thoughts racing, Quintin struggled to find a solution. *Gotta take him in. No choice.* After a moment, Quintin picked him up and noticed the little guy had stopped breathing. "Oh no! Oh no!" he cried. "What have I done to you?" His little body was now limp and lifeless. Quintin held him in his hands as his tears freely flowed. "Sorry. I'm so sorry," he kept repeating.

Several hours later, he wrapped the puppy in the little blanket and buried his little friend in an unmarked area. It took Quintin several days to leave his apartment.

His nearby friends heard the news from his roommate and tried to encourage him, but Quintin could not be comforted. He said, "He was my responsibility and my friend, and I let him down."

Two weeks later, Quintin visited the breeder and informed him of what had happened.

"They all died—every one of them from that litter. Other families have come by with their news over the last several days. It was parvo," the breeder told Quintin.

It was the first time the virus had struck home and made its mark on Quintin. He'd had other dogs while growing up, and none had come down with the terrible disease.

"I have another litter recently weaned, and I've got one left. He's yours if you want him."

Quintin looked up at him from staring at the dirt. "May I see him? Is he healthy?"

"Yes, had them all vaccinated this time."

Quintin looked into the small box and noticed a tiny pup yelping for dear life. It was also tricolored, with less brown and more black and white. Quintin took the new pup home, quickly had him assessed by the vet's office, and named him Rocket.

"Calm down," Quintin told him as Rocket panted heavily in the summer heat. Now twelve months old, his pup looked at him and continued panting while saliva went everywhere. Quintin had put a small water bowl on the floor mat, and the pooch would lap up a few gulps only to spread the water everywhere, adding to the copious amounts of wet, foamy drool on the backseat, passenger seat, and dash.

After a couple of hours of the mess, frustrated, Quintin pulled off the side of the road, where he noticed a nearby canal. With Rocket's heavy panting and excessive anxiety, Quintin worried he might collapse from heatstroke. Without giving it much thought, he grabbed Rocket, picked him up, and threw him into the canal. The water was deeper than he'd thought, causing the dog to go underwater longer than he had expected. A few seconds later, Rocket popped up like a cork and swam back to the canal bank. Quintin picked him up, placed him in the backseat, and drove off.

Now back on the road, Quintin glanced in the rearview mirror and noticed Rocket was shivering with a disgusted look of disapproval at what had just transpired. Moments later, his four-legged buddy fell asleep for the duration of the trip. "Sorry, buddy, but you were driving me crazy. You'll be okay." He took one last look at Rocket. *Good. No more drooling*, he thought.

Arriving home in Hialeah was always welcoming and this time was special because of the closing of one chapter in his life and, hopefully, the beginning of a new one. Quintin's mom always had a warm smile and plenty of hugs whenever her children returned home. His father was warm but somewhat formal.

Rocket was always happy to see them, but the feeling was not quite mutual. Milva distrusted canines. As a young girl in Cuba, she had been bitten by a local dog and had to have painful rabies vaccinations. It was a traumatic event she never forgot.

Ciso, who'd been raised on a farm, treated animals with little to no emotion. *"Hijo, animales no son gente."* He would constantly remind his children that animals were not people. It was not unlike him to occasionally shove the dog aside. He would do that with any dog if it was aggravating him. One afternoon, while Ciso slept on the couch, Rocket approached him, and before Quintin could stop him, the dog licked his father right in his slightly opened mouth. Ciso awoke and struck Rocket on the head, sending the pooch crying and running away.

"Dad, why did you hit him? He was just giving you affection."

Ciso's disapproval was obvious. "Disgusting! Absolutely disgusting. I'm not about to let some dog lick me, least of all in my mouth."

Quintin coddled his buddy, even though no real harm had been done. He laughed at Rocket's reaction to the situation. Unfazed, Ciso ignored both of them and walked out into the backyard.

Hialeah, Florida, in the mid-1980s was growing exponentially. Many minority groups were arriving each year, bringing their distinct cultures with them. Just five years earlier, the Mariel boatlift had brought thousands of Cubans in a mass exodus. Many exiled family members from the 1960s were able to cross the Florida Straits on private vessels to retrieve family in Cuba. During that time, the Cuban government forced incarcerated Cubans to board flotilla boats along with the requested family members. The captains of the vessels were given an ultimatum: "Take what we give you, or else the requested persons will not be allowed to leave." These prisoners were neither asked for nor welcomed by the exiled Cuban community in the United States or any other American citizens. They became known as *Marielitos,* a derogatory term implying those who came from Cuba in the boatlift were degenerates. They were initially welcomed, even if with some apprehension, and were given the opportunity to work and acclimate to American society. However, just a few short years later, many were quickly branded lazy, entitled, and inconsiderate, and scores of them were incarcerated for a host of crimes, hence the negative connotation of their nickname. Many of them opted to return to Cuba.

"Why someone would want to return to that shithole is beyond my comprehension," Ciso said. "The spirit of the Cuban people is broken. They are hopeless, godless, and without freedom and hope. Their economy, ever worsening, has created a society that just concentrates on existence. Their future is bleak."

Few would have argued. Life on the Island was distressing. Few realized that after the breakup of the Soviet Union several years later, with the resulting diminished aid to the island, their plight was about to get much worse.

"I've missed you," Cari said.

"I missed you too," said Quintin.

Cari was now a sophomore in high school. Quintin tried to keep his emotions in check. *She's fifteen!* He kept reminding himself. Still, when he looked at her, he couldn't help his feelings. When their eyes met, he felt certain that the connection was mutual. He studied every inch of her face. Her straight, long hair with bangs and her warm smile made her irresistible to him. She had beautiful dark eyes and thin lips and was petite and slim. But it wasn't just her physical attributes he admired. Always pleasant and encouraging, she wore confidence like a comfortable old T-shirt. She had an unusual peace about her that had been evident since he met her.

"Congratulations on your graduation," she said.

"Thanks. Campus life was closing in on me. I can't wait to start AOCS later this summer," he responded.

Quintin was eventually allowed to visit Cari at her home in East Hialeah but only under the watchful eyes of someone in her family. Her mother, Marcia, had divorced their biological father five years earlier and had met Levi, a coworker, during that time. After a short courtship, they married. She was Catholic, and he was Jewish. Their courtship had begun with their seeing each other in private, for fear of a family backlash. Levi had also endured a recent nasty divorce himself.

Cari lived with her parents and her younger sister, Isabel, in an upstairs duplex, while Marcia's aging parents lived downstairs. Arman and his wife, China, had fled Cuba before the revolution. They'd lived in Boston, Massachusetts, for a couple of years before moving to Miami in order to avoid the harsh winters.

It didn't take long for Quintin to feel welcomed by her parents and grandparents, but he made sure he always remained in line. He knew he was a hair's breadth away from retribution. Over the next several weeks, he came to see Cari as often as allowed. Quintin soon realized her confidence and peace stemmed from her faith.

"I gave my life to Christ when I was eleven," she told him. "Do you believe?"

Quintin pondered for a moment. The words did not seem to come easily to him. "I'm not certain," he admitted.

"Jesus claims to be the Son of God. Do you believe that? Do you think this is true?" she asked.

"I'm just not sure. Besides, somebody's truth may not be someone else's."

"There can only be one truth," she responded. "I also know God loves you."

Their conversations about God and faith always got

him thinking. He had a lot to process and think about. That night, he took her small hand in his, and after a moment that he wished could last longer, he slowly released it and made his way back to the car. "See ya soon."

"Okay," she said.

On the ten-minute drive to his parents' house, he couldn't help but think about the deep words she'd shared with him but also the unflinching confidence in her demeanor. Later that evening, he called her to say good night and also to ask her out on their first unescorted date. He was tired of dragging her pesky sister along with them. He would have to find the courage to ask her parents the next time he saw them.

The following day, while at home, Quintin listened to his new favorite tape. Several months prior, he had seen the movie *Top Gun* and bought the soundtrack on cassette. He played it over and over, much to the displeasure of his father, who constantly objected to the loud music, claiming it was about to make him deaf. "*Baja eso. Me vas a poner sordo.*"

After he lowered the volume, Quintin's thoughts returned to flying jet fighters off carriers, since the movie was about naval aviation.

His mother, Milva, was on summer break from teaching at the nearby elementary school, where she had been working for several years. Her ability to work all day, prepare every meal, clean dishes, and manage the family home with Quintin and his sister day in and day out was impressive. In the Cuban culture, moms were sacred. Her example to them left a strong impression as to what hard work and dedication to family looked like. Margret and Quintin strove to emulate that strong ethic with their families.

"*Es hora de comer. Llama a tu padre.*"

Quintin called his father to dinner. Ciso had been working on the backhoe currently parked on the side of the yard. Ciso worked hard in construction, primarily with heavy equipment. He was a thin, tough, and stubborn man. Eighteen years had passed since they left Cuba. He had a strong work ethic outside the home. "Men work outside the home, and women work inside," he often said, as if certain cultural customs were supposed to be in place and not questioned. Quintin and his sister often thought he had it easier than their mom did.

The smell of rice and black beans, *pollo asado*, and fried plantains wafted through the whole house. In their home, the jalousie windows and broken screens were an open invitation to flies and mosquitoes. Without air-conditioning, fans were the only relief from the heat and humidity of South Florida. Every afternoon, Quintin would grab the flyswatter and hunt for invading flies throughout the house. He got adept at eliminating the little critters; however, mosquitoes proved to be more difficult foes.

Milva was quiet that evening. It was the fifth anniversary of the passing of her youngest brother, Ozzie. He'd died from a blood clot, his caregiver had said. Milva had an old family friend named Luisa who still lived in her hometown and had offered to take care of him after her aging aunt Liche died fourteen months before Ozzie. When Liche passed, Milva was able to travel to Cuba through the Red Cross to make arrangements for her funeral and arrange care for Ozzie. Luisa's help during that time was invaluable. Liche was buried in the town cemetery next to Milva's parents, Luis and Micaela. No one else was in attendance. Having no surviving family and with most of her generation gone, Liche was truly alone. Milva placed a few gardenias on each of their graves. She cried and prayed a little but mostly cried.

"*Hola, consorte. ¿Dime algo brode?*"

"*Hola, Eddie. ¿Cómo estás?*" responded Ciso.

Many Cubans had adopted a form of Cubanism Spanish. Like Ebonics for English or slang for any language, it was a common street form of identification that left no doubt of one's background. *Consorte* meant "companion" or "buddy," while *brode* was "brother." The best example of Cubanism Spanish was the word *ño*. It could mean anything. It came to describe whatever emotion or intention one had. For example, "*Ño!*" with strong intonation or tone signified surprise or astonishment. It could represent anger, disgust, exhilaration, lust, and more. The two-letter word, originally short for *coño* (*damn*), was used commonly and understood by all in the Cuban community.

The heat was now in full force, and any shade was welcomed. Eddie was a distant cousin who had come from Cuba ten years prior and had learned English on the streets and in workplaces in Miami. He never had gotten beyond the eighth grade after dropping out to support his family, which consisted of multiple generations in one home. Not all were family; some were close friends who needed a place to stay. Among the Cubans, *cousin* came to mean anyone closely aligned with one's cultural norms and values, whether he or she was related or not.

"Well, I know things are going to change on the island. The Soviet Union cannot keep supporting the Castro regime. This president will see to their downfall. Go Reagan!" Eddie was not shy about politics and was always vocal. An able debater, he seemed to have many facts in his verbal armada; however, time after time, some of the facts were not accurate. In fact, Ciso felt that Eddie saw the world around him how he thought it should be and not how it truly was.

"*No creo. Los Americanos* are not going to send troops to overthrow Castro," responded Ciso.

"Oh, come on. They did it to Noriega, and the CIA has been doing it to other countries for years. Besides, you will be able to get your father's land back. From what your brother tells me, you have Felix's property title with you," responded Eddie.

"Island Cubans are not just going to hand over those properties after so many years, *chico*. Those property titles are from the Batista era. The Castro regime is gonna wipe their asses with them," Quintin said.

"*Hay, no joda, si eso pasa entonces hay que arrancar cabeza*," concluded Eddie.

Ciso and Quintin stayed quiet for a moment. Quintin wondered how many others in their family circle thought that way, let alone in the entire exiled community.

"The Americans will not support a revolution on the island, Eddie. Does the Bay of Pigs mean anything to you?" responded Ciso, starting to get irritated, as he often did with what he considered ridiculous political perceptions.

The conversation continued for almost an hour with both sides entrenched. They went on trying to prove their respective points without giving the opposing side any validity. They were sitting around the dinner table in such deep conversation that neither of them heard a knock. Moments later, Lipio made his appearance. "*Caballeros, buenas tardes*," he said, instantly realizing there was another testy political discussion going on by the looks on Ciso's, Eddie's, and Quintin's faces. Lipio helped himself to a cold café, hoping to hear more of the subject and get in on the debate.

All the while, Quintin was grateful his mother was not present. With her fiery Barcelona lineage, the temperature in the room would invariably have headed in only one direction, and the situation would have ended badly.

"*Bueno, me tengo que ir.*" Eddie rose to leave after finishing his now cold *cafecito*. "*Ño,* I hate cold café. *Hasta luego primo,*" he added as he headed for the door.

"Okay, *chico,*" responded Ciso. As they watched Eddie drive away, Quintin rose from his chair and started to head out as well. "*Yo quiero ese muchacho pero, el es un come mierda,*" his father said. "Everyone needs to move on and let go of the past. The Cuba we knew and remember is gone and will never come back."

"Dad, a lot of people think like he does. The Cuban revolution was a lie, and many people were fooled. Besides, maybe there's some truth in what he's saying that a revolution might be needed," Quintin said.

Ciso just glared at his son with eyes wide open, surprised by his son's statement. "*O cara!*" He abruptly got up from the table and walked back to the yard. The thought of a war, any war, was "the greatest failure in the human race," his father often said. Now, with his son planning on military service, it was unthinkable.

Lipio gave Quintin a wink and followed Ciso into the yard.

"Sounds like I missed one hell of a political discussion," Lipio said.

"No, not really. Eddie's just young and idealistic, and so is Quintin, for that matter," replied Ciso.

"Remind you of anyone?" responded Lipio as he stared and smiled at his longtime friend.

"*O cara*, must you remind me of those days?" said Ciso. "By the way, what's the latest news on your son and the events on the island?"

"That's part of the reason I'm here," replied Lipio. Ciso, over the last ten years, had learned that Lipio's old flame Carla was separated from her husband and wished to get the young boy out of the country. Carla insisted the now eleven-year-old boy, Ivancito, was Lipio's. She had secretly arranged for the boy to be smuggled through Honduras. There Lipio would make arrangements to pick him up and drive across the southern Texas border. Sometime later, Carla would attempt the same.

"It's been arranged. My plan is to drive down to Honduras in the next several days, and I'll make contact for specifics with Carla's amigos in Honduras," added Lipio. "Some of the expenses were paid on her end. Most of the cost, however, will be on my end, given the poor value of the Cuban peso. My understanding is that these smugglers want US dollars. Can you cover my work obligations with the backhoe while I'm gone?"

"*Claro*, but how long do you think this will take? By the way, who are these so-called friends?" asked Ciso.

"Not sure. Never met any of them. Carla seems to

know more since she has visited the country several times in the past ten years. In either case, I'm not sure about another option. I looked into an attorney who sympathizes with the plight of the Cubans, and he was too expensive."

"Where's the boy now?" asked Ciso.

"My guess is, he's being transported sometime this weekend when he's out of school. I need to be able to go as soon as they give the signal." Lipio rose to leave, thanked Ciso again, and said he would call him as soon as he left.

"*Ten cuidado, mi hermano*," replied Ciso.

***

"My family and I would like to invite you to church tonight. Will you come?" asked an enthusiastic Cari over the phone. "They're even letting me ride with you, and then you can drop me off after."

"Sounds good," Quintin responded.

"Pick me up around six. Church starts at six thirty."

As they hung up, Quintin was excited and looking forward to spending time alone with her, even if it was a church date. The next few hours seemed to fly. That afternoon, Quintin's two buddies came over to discuss plans for a short cruise to start the summer with a bang.

Quintin had met Paulo when they were both in middle school. Known for his rugged looks, Paulo was charismatic, outgoing, and a great dancer. The girls always went wild over him. Randy was a few years older.

He was intelligent and a natural prankster. He'd graduated from engineering school recently and was now working for Florida Power and Light, the electric company. Quintin loved and respected them both. Their friendship defied distance, personal conflict, and loss and would endure well into the future. Three brothers from different mothers, they had formed a tight-knit group that even many natural siblings did not have.

"So are you gonna tell us about this girl who seems to consume your every thought?" asked Randy.

"What girl?" Quintin responded.

"Don't! Don't even try to deny it, dude!" Paulo said. "We've heard about some young girl you've been seeing. Your sister filled us in."

Great, Quintin thought. He tried to downplay the relationship, but Paulo and Randy knew him too well, and Quintin knew there was no getting out of it. "Well, we met last year. Remember when I was a lifeguard at the city pool? We met there. It was weird, guys. I didn't think it would last this long. There is something special about her," Quintin said. As he tried to keep his answers brief and fairly vague, eventually, they asked about her age.

"She's *what*? Fifteen! Are you stupid, or are you stupid?" asked Randy.

Paulo partly smiled, and the conversation went downhill from there. "She's jailbait. What are you going to do—take her to Chuck E. Cheese's?" His friends were having too much fun with this. "Chester the molester." More laughter ensued.

Quintin picked up Cari in his Bug, and off they went to church. The ride was mostly quiet but pleasant. They both had stupid grins on their faces, which was typical whenever they were together. The sermon that night was direct and deep. Forgiveness, putting others first, and praying for one's enemies were hard concepts for Quintin to grasp, and he pondered their meaning for some time. He struggled that night, knowing military service had a completely different philosophy. He didn't have all the answers then, but he knew he couldn't confuse the two. He was going to have to balance military life and a Christian life. *I'm going to be trained to kill others, and the pastor is talking about forgiveness and praying for our enemies. I don't know how that's possible*, he thought.

When church ended that night, Cari asked Quintin for a small favor. "Before you take me home, can we take Alex home?" she asked.

"Well, okay, I guess," Quintin responded hesitantly. His annoyance grew as he thought more about it. *Why is she asking me to take her ex-boyfriend home?*

During the ride from church, Quintin noticed she was grinning. He was not. *I sure hope she's not playing games like so many other girls do. If she is, that crap ain't gonna stand.* He had dated other girls before and was fed up with petty, emotional tug-of-war games.

After they dropped off Alex, Cari suggested they stop at a nearby ice cream shop not far from the church. After they arrived, she ordered her favorite, orange sherbet, while he went for the butter pecan. As they sat in the car and finished their cold treats, Quintin finally got around to asking her why she'd asked him to give her ex-boyfriend a ride home.

"I knew we could spend a little more time alone since we had to drop him off," she said.

"Oh," he said, somewhat stunned by her conniving little plan.

As they looked at each other, Gato Barbieri's "Europa" was playing on the radio, and he slowly leaned over and kissed her left cheek. Nervous and with his heart racing yet undaunted, he then gently kissed her on the lips. After a seemingly eternal three seconds, she backed off, in fear of going further.

"We shouldn't be. I shouldn't be ..."

He started to explain, when she suddenly turned in her chair, reached over, took his head in her hands, and said, "It'll be okay." She then kissed him deeply. Her kiss was sweet and profound. Pressed against the seat, he had never experienced anything like that before.

After he dropped her off that evening, there was no doubt in his mind he was falling in love with her.

The following weekend, her grandparents Arman and China were celebrating a relative's birthday, and Fe's family was invited for the festivities, which included a traditional pig roast. Ciso and Milva were apprehensive at first, but after a little arm twisting by their son, they agreed to attend. Besides, Cuban pig roasts were hard to pass up. The tradition went back many generations. The guest of honor was usually selected based on its size, assuming the breeder was well known for raising good hogs. The old way of slaughtering the poor creature involved taking a knife to the heart for a seemingly quick death. However, it was not unusual for a hog to stand back up again and run around the pen, screaming and bleeding, during its final moments. Not having been raised on farms, Quintin and most of his generation were not used to that. They disliked some of the old ways and preferred more humane methods, such as buying the animal at the grocery store, already prepared. Fortunately, the local breeders also had a processing plant, which simplified the ordeal, making it as painless as possible for the humans. They'd choose the victim and, after a short while, pick it up in a box. That left the *sazon* and roasting to their patrons. That process was often contested too. Traditionalists argued that a hole in the ground was the only way to roast the pig. Others opted for the *caja* China, or Chinese box, a metallic box placed over the grill that roasted the pig with radiant heat, similar to an oven. Arman had built a brick oven and preferred to roast the hog over briquettes while slowly turning the meat. "The hole in the ground is too much work, and with a *caja* China, there's no way of smoking the meat," he said. They still argued about the preferred way.

The guests arrived, always fashionably late. It was said that as a Cuban, if one arrived on time, he or she was two hours early. One might have thought to suggest moving the official time earlier, but it wouldn't have made a difference; somehow, everyone seemed to know what time the host really meant. The scene was often festive and borderline chaotic. Cubans, and Latin people in general, seemed to all speak at the same time, especially the ladies. How they could understand each other always puzzled Quintin.

China, highly respected and loved by the family, was the matriarch. She commanded respect with her endless love and a servant's heart. In her early eighties, she had been babysitting toddlers and preschool children for little to no pay for most of her adult life. She felt it was her ministry, and she enjoyed loving on those kids. She loved having family and friends over; however, when she was ready for them to leave, she would let them know by taking a glass of water and sprinkling her guests with her hand while saying, "*Calabaza, calabaza cada uno pa' su casa.*" The English translation did not rhyme, but it meant essentially "It's time for everyone to go home as water is sprinkled on your face." She was so loved that no one was ever offended.

At the pig roast, the men in the family watched Quintin closely but kept their distance. Quintin introduced Cari to his father. She'd already met his mother at her fifteenth birthday three months earlier. Milva was obviously taken by her. Ciso was polite but distant as they formally hugged in the cultural tradition. "He," Ciso said, pointing to his son, "can't stop talking about you."

"Dad!" replied an embarrassed Quintin. They all smiled, and Ciso chuckled the loudest.

The women in her family were curious and kind. Quintin understood the tension but felt welcomed somewhat. Ciso and Milva seemed at ease and were immediately involved in endless conversations about the plight of Cuban refugees and how they made it to those shores. Sacrifice, suffering, and loss touched each family. The Communist revolution in Cuba was an exposed nerve. Many still had ties to the island through relatives and close friends who still lived there. Communication with the island continued to be difficult due to technical issues and high costs. Telephone conversations were not easy to come by, so they were usually short and to the point. Milva made calls mostly to make sure her older brother's two children were getting along as best as they could. Sending aid through third-party carriers was common. Milva regularly sent financial assistance to them through Western Union. Some in the Cuban exile community were critical of any monetary assistance, fearing the funds would aid the Communist government and prolong their grip on power.

"*Idiotas!*" Milva often said in quick rebuttal. "My brother and my entire family died down there. I'm just trying to help what's left of my family."

A few years after the Mariel boatlift, two of Arman's nephews had built a makeshift raft and taken to the Florida Straits. Upon arriving in the Florida Keys several days later, they were processed at the Krome Detention Center until claimed by family. The men were thin and exhausted but alive. Several of their companions in another raft weren't as fortunate. Exactly how many lost their lives while crossing the straits would never be known, but estimates were in the thousands. Most left for similar reasons. Food, household goods, wood, metal, and petroleum were hard to come by. Automobiles and parts for anything mechanical were practically nonexistent. In addition to the scarcity and lack of basic provisions on the island, something important was still missing to Ciso, something he never heard about from the second wave of refugees: freedom. No one claimed their motivation for leaving the island was to be free, to make and plan their futures as they saw fit, and to express their opinions openly without fear of retribution. To him, those were nonnegotiable and essential. He had seen his generation flourish in the midst of challenges when they arrived in the United States. He claimed that independence from institutions and the opportunity to pursue economic prosperity were by-products of that philosophy. Meanwhile, the newer generation were becoming more dependent on those same institutions to provide for them instead of making a living for themselves.

"Many Cubans have turned to welfare, food stamps, and the like rather than sacrificing and working hard," he said. "Bunch of lazy bums, entitled and with unappreciative attitudes." To him, freedom was all that was needed. It was as precious as life itself. It was worth the sacrifice and losses he and his family had endured in order to attain it and hold on to it.

"*Buenas tardes*, Arman. *Me llamo* Ciso."

"Oh, *muy bien en conocerte*," responded Cari 's grandfather.

They discussed family and life issues, including work, places lived, and their overall experiences in the United States. Cari's grandparents, along with Cari's mother, first lived in Boston after they left the island in 1957. The winters were harsh, so they opted to move to South Florida. Arman, now that he had become better acquainted with Ciso, felt at ease in sharing about the loss of one of his eight brothers during the revolution. Ciso listened intently as Arman described what he knew.

"It was right after the revolution. Castro had seized power, and details are scarce, but my brother Nicolas was accused of aiding the attempted downfall of Fidel.

My brother was a chauffeur for one of Batista's generals. The general fled the country when he heard Batista had abdicated. My brother and one hundred fifty other men were arrested. At first, they were going to be released, but word had it Raul Castro, Fidel's brother, caught wind of all this. Next thing I knew, there was a speedy trial, and the following day, they were all executed. It was all a lie. My brother was thirty-four, kind, and apolitical. If they needed to arrest anyone, it should've been me. We left in '57 because we knew Castro was bad news. We tried warning friends and family, but to no avail."

"Did they arrest him at his home, or what happened?" asked Ciso.

"No, he was riding from Havana to Pinar del Río, when he was taken from a bus. We got word he was defiant, so they beat him before the trial and sentencing." Arman showed him a picture of his brother. "I don't know if it's true, but we heard a woman on the bus tried to help, and she was slapped or beaten—I'm not sure. In any case, that's what the bus driver said. He was an acquaintance of ours who was from my hometown."

Ciso, now expressionless, was unable to speak. His thoughts raced with memories of his experience many years earlier on a bus. *That bus,* he thought. "Those were dark days, Arman. I didn't heed the warnings either. My in-laws tried to warn us of what they saw so clearly. My idealism got in the way of reason. I was hoping for a better

165

Cuba with the promise of the revolution, and instead, we lost our country to ruthless demagogy backed by a Soviet safety net."

"*Y donde estaban los Americanos*?" Arman asked.

Ciso also felt somewhat betrayed by the United States. "After the promise of support and the subsequent betrayal during the Bay of Pigs, Castro was handed a military and propaganda gift. In any case, we, not the Americans, lost our country, amigo," Ciso said.

The festivities lasted into the early evening. Later, back at their home, Quintin asked his parents what they thought of Cari.

"She seems very sweet," said his mother.

"Coqui," said his father, "she's only fifteen!"

"I know," Quintin responded. "But she's different. I can feel it!"

His father's only response was "*O cara.*"

Several days passed, when Milva received a phone call asking for Ciso. The caller said it was urgent, and when Milva informed him her husband was not home, he asked for Ciso to call back as soon as possible. She tried to get more information; however, the caller gave no details, only a callback number.

When Ciso arrived home, he received the message and immediately called. Milva, fearing bad news by the tone of the caller's voice several hours earlier, stared at her husband as his face grew pale. *Hay Dios, que habra pasado?* she wondered as she watched him in the back room from the living room.

Ciso sat quietly listening, and moments later, he dropped the phone onto the couch. He rose, slowly walked out to the back porch, and sat on the metal outdoor furniture. He seemed to stare at a bougainvillea bush in front of him, not really seeing its beautiful red flowers and sharp thorns. "I told him not to go. Told him not to go!" he kept repeating.

Milva joined him outside and sat down across from him. After a short but seemingly long moment, she asked what had happened. He had confided in her about Lipio's trip to Honduras several days earlier. The caller had been Vicente Torres, an old acquaintance of theirs from Pinar del Río. Vicente had moved his family and several close friends and coworkers to Honduras in the late 1960s to start growing Cuban seed tobacco in the hope of selling internationally. Over the years, he and his team had done well and had loose ties to Cuba.

The plan, as set up by Carla months earlier, had been to have Ivancito brought onto Vicente's tobacco farm and make the exchange once payment was delivered. Everything was going well. One of Vicente's coworkers, his trusted foreman, was present to make sure they could get into the building. Just after sundown, they met at Vicente's admin office adjacent to the cigar house on his farm.

Lipio was pleased to see the boy for the first time. "He looks like his mother," Lipio said. Realizing the eleven-year-old was apprehensive about the current situation, Lipio tried to assure him that all was well. The mood was tense but straightforward. After Lipio confirmed his identity to the two smugglers, they quickly asked for payment. Lipio handed them the agreed-upon amount of $6,600.

One of the two smugglers was shorter and thinner than his partner and did all the talking. He wore a long-sleeved plaid shirt, white denim slacks, and western-style boots. His hat was made of white straw, and he wore it low on his brow, as if to conceal his face. The taller fellow was heavyset, with sunken eyes, and his nose seemed too small for his face. He wore black jeans, old high-top blue Converse sneakers, and a long-sleeved polyester shirt that was too small for his build.

"*¡Son diez mil!*" said the short, thin smuggler.

"*Como?*" asked a surprised Lipio.

"That's right. It's ten thousand dollars. We told Carla there were expenses, and the cost has gone up."

"I brought the agreed-upon amount—no more, no less," Lipio said.

"*Vamonos*, Rubio." The shorter man signaled to his partner to leave, revealing his partner's name.

"*Esperate*! I can get the rest. I just need to gather what I can. Give me a day or two. *Por favor.* This is my son.

I've come a long way," Lipio responded, now concerned all his effort would fall apart.

Vicente was not clear on what had happened next. The young Ivancito cried and tried to break free from his escort, when Lipio leaped forward and tried to free the child. Rubio, the larger smuggler, intercepted Lipio in the process, and now both men were physically involved. According to Vicente's foreman, Lipio knocked Rubio to the ground with relative ease. The usually jovial Cuban hillbilly was exceptionally strong thanks to a life of hard work on the farm and was not easily angered. Those who knew him knew to stay clear of him, for fear his wrath would be unleashed.

As Lipio turned his attention once again to the other smuggler holding Ivancito, he was confronted with a small revolver that had been concealed. Lipio, in a fury, either didn't see or didn't care about the gun being pointed at him, and he approached the smaller smuggler. The foreman, seeing the weapon, ran toward the door, not looking back. He heard two shots, possibly three, as he exited the small building, running for his life.

About an hour later, Vicente, his foreman, and several workmen returned to the admin building. They found Lipio lying on his side, motionless. He apparently had died from the gunshot wounds but not before dragging himself another twenty feet toward the door. The smugglers and the young boy Ivancito were nowhere to be found.

Ciso finished relaying the caller's information to Milva, and it was a few minutes before either one could utter a word. They realized they had lost the closest of friends. To Ciso, Lipio had been more than a friend; he had been his brother. *How? Why?* he thought.

Ciso slowly rose from his seat, got in his car, and drove away. Several hours later, Margret and Quintin arrived home and learned the terrible news.

The following day, Ciso returned home. No one knew what he'd done or where he had gone. Aside from several distant cousins and a few friends, Lipio had no one else. Lipio's backhoe stayed on the property for several years before Ciso finally came around to selling it for parts.

CHAPTER 13

Anytime, Anywhere, 1993

"Rampage 205, this is Tower. You are cleared for takeoff. Runway 260. Assume Alpha route, and contact departure on 207.3."

"Roger. Clear." Quintin pushed the throttles into full military thrust, and the Tomcat B roared to life and quickly picked up speed down the runway. The B model delivered substantially more thrust than its predecessor, the A model. In fact, F-14 Bs were able to take off from carriers and airfields without afterburner, which gave them more fuel and precious airborne time.

"All systems looked good," Quintin said as he quickly scanned his instruments. As the fighter accelerated down the runway, he slowly pulled back on the stick, and a moment later, the Tomcat was airborne. With gear and flaps up, he pulled back the throttles to maintain departure speed and avoid excessive noise over the densely populated areas west of the air base. Miramar Naval Air Station was the home of fighter aviation for the navy on the West Coast of the United States. Many of the local residents welcomed the sound of freedom, but others did not and frequently called the base to complain about the noisy jet jocks. *Why in the world would anyone buy a home next to an active jet base? Who knows?* thought Quintin. He and Brice, his radar intercept officer (RIO), call sign Doc, had flown together many times in the past, especially during Operation Desert Storm and Operation Desert Shield just eighteen months prior.

Arriving in the Persian Gulf right after the ceasefire in 1991, the air wing stationed aboard USS *Nimitz* (CVN-68) was to protect the civilian Kurds in the north of Iraq. Iraqi forces were brutalizing the Kurdish people and probably would've annihilated them in a few months. In addition, the air wing was to maintain a no-fly zone over the country and deny Saddam Hussein any tactical air capabilities. Arriving on station after six weeks spent transiting the wide and beautiful Pacific as well as the northern part of the Indian Ocean, the sailors and crew were ready for what might come. Well trained and eager, the young warriors couldn't wait to get into the action. Some of the fighter pilots were disappointed they had not been there when hostilities and the shock and awe started. However, they soon found out that even though a ceasefire had been declared, many Iraqi forces were still in full combat mode, and some were undoubtedly eager to possibly down one of the US air assets, knowing the rules of engagement applied unilaterally.

Once they entered through the Strait of Hormuz, the horizon over the sea took on a gray haze. Visibility was cut down in all directions. Topside on the flight deck, the constant smell of burned fuel was toxic, especially to the eyes and lungs. *What a difference*, thought Quintin. For several weeks of transiting the oceans, the point where the sky met the sea on the horizon had been crisp and beautiful. Quintin's thoughts turned to the wooden caravel explorers used in the past centuries. He thought of Magellan crossing the Pacific and circumnavigating the globe with his tiny craft and dwindling small fleet. *It must've been awesome yet brutal in hardship and loss*, he thought. *So many of his men were lost at sea. Stretches the imagination.* He also thought of the great English explorer Captain James Cook, who'd discovered the Great Barrier Reef of Australia only to meet his doom on the Hawaiian Islands at the hands of the natives. *Crazy bastards*, he said to himself.

Now Quintin and his crewmates were there on a modern-day aircraft carrier more than three football fields long and made not of wood but of steel, an entire air wing of murderous aircraft capable of delivering over-the-horizon death and destruction to the recipient.

The flight deck was usually crammed yet orderly, arranged with S-3 Viking antisubmarine aircraft, A-6 Intruder bombers, F/A-18 Hornet fighter bombers, E-2 Hawkeye radars, and EA-6 electronic warfare jammers. Then there was the COD, a propeller craft used by the navy to ferry personnel and cargo to and from the ship. It was the ugliest aircraft Quintin had ever seen, yet it was practical, efficient, and a sight for sore eyes in anticipation of mail delivery from home.

Finally, there was Quintin's heartthrob, the aircraft he dreamed of flying: the F-14 Tomcat. It was large for a fighter yet agile enough not only to intercept incoming enemy bombers, its original purpose, but also to hold its own in a dogfight, or a knife fight, as it was referred to. When the wings were fully swept back in the delta configuration, it appeared like the tip of an arrow or spear. Fast, it was slick and sexy, the crew said. Yet when flying aboard the ship, the F-14 had to slow down enough not to overstress the arrestment wire on the deck or the landing gear on the aircraft or damage anything in its path. It was nicknamed the Turkey while in that configuration, as it waddled and swayed from side to side and up and down. It was challenging to master, and as with anything difficult to achieve, the payoff was greater.

One of the most difficult scenarios to perform was single-engine flight operation, especially when trying to land. The engines were nine feet apart, and the asymmetry of their thrust when one engine was out could easily overtake the pilot. That was accentuated at slower speeds, such as on landings. On a ten-thousand-foot runway, it was difficult. On a moving platform at sea, with little room for error, to the crew, it was nearly impossible.

One sunny afternoon, Quintin's former roommate experienced engine difficulty on a routine mission. The pilot and his RIO had an engine flameout and were unable to restart it. The ship was in blue water operations, which technically meant no divert field and no long runway available. All the ship's company and air-wing personnel were on hand to witness the event. Some of the guys took bets on whether the crew would make it safely aboard, eject at sea, or die trying. Navy fighter pilots held nothing sacred.

Quintin was nervous, and the thought of his friend dying was gut-wrenching. *Come on, Lynch. Do this!* he thought.

The Tomcat's nose swung left and right as the throttle was adjusted. Wing-down top rudder was a usual flying technique, which meant good engine down, opposite wing up, and judicious use of rudder. Everyone held his breath for the last eighteen seconds of the landing sequence. On final approach, they had to stay in the groove and proceed with utmost precision or else. Adding full throttle to abort and go around for another landing was not a good option, least of all with a single engine. At three-quarters of a mile, they called the ball.

"Roger ball," the LSO said.

Getting underpowered on final during the last eighteen seconds before a landing was the most critical. If they got underpowered, it was highly unlikely they would have the thrust to abort the landing and go around for another attempt. Losing control of the Tomcat so close to the ship's stern would most likely yield catastrophic damage of epic proportions. With the possibility of the ensuing explosion and fireball, everyone aboard had a high pucker factor, especially the brave souls on the flight deck. Quintin and his squadron mates knew all too well after witnessing what could happen in those horrible accidents.

It wasn't the most beautiful landing, but they walked out of their aircraft after arresting the barricade the ship's personnel had set up across the flight deck. All breathed a sigh of relief. Lynch later said, "I wouldn't wish that experience on my worst enemy." For exemplary flying, he was awarded an air medal. There were no arguments to that, although most of the pilots, deep inside, felt they could've done a better job. Quintin was no exception.

Taking off from the flight deck was mind- and body-wrenching. They went from zero to 160 miles per hour in two and a half seconds on those steam catapults. Quintin always thought of his first cat shot aboard the *Lexington* almost four years prior. Nothing was that wicked, he concluded.

Once they took off from the ship, the nasty smoke and haze in all directions ended around two thousand feet of altitude. "Nice," Quintin told his RIO in the backseat through the intercom. "It's great to see blue sky again, Doc."

Brice looked ahead and upward and nodded in agreement.

Most of the missions flown over Iraq were combat air patrols. The briefed missions were long, up to five hours, requiring in-flight refueling twice: once en route to their predetermined airspace and then once more upon returning to the ship. Almost all the flights were at night. They were always in a flight-of-two configuration called a section. Quintin was the wingman since he was a relatively new pilot, with an experienced RIO in the backseat, and the other fighter was an experienced flight lead, usually with a junior RIO.

That night started like many others. They headed northwest over the Persian Gulf, turned slightly more westerly over Kuwait, and then rendezvoused with the KC-135 tanker for the stressful in-flight refueling. The tanker had a long boom that telescoped under and behind it to allow adjoining aircraft to approach it slowly. A boom operator maneuvered the telephone-pole tube to attach it to the approaching aircraft, usually just behind the receiving aircraft's cockpit. At least that was the way the air force did it. For the navy, a six-foot rubber extension resembling a fireman's hose was attached at the end of the pole, with a metal basket to receive the plug from the fuel-recipient aircraft. Each pilot had to carefully approach the basket and fly formation on the tanker while eyeing the basket on the right side of the cockpit with his peripheral vision. The pucker factor was always high during those maneuvers. When things went wrong—and they did—it was not uncommon to have the metal basket whip across and strike the canopy when the probe missed while they attempted to plug it. That often led to cracked canopies and a basket torn off completely due to pilot-induced oscillations. The torn-off basket sometimes entered the right engine nacelle, which was always catastrophic. The metal basket would strike the jet engine's steel compressor blades, which destroyed the engine in an explosion with a subsequent ball of fire and invariably led to loss of the aircraft and the crew with it.

"Are you ready for this plug, Quintin?" asked an inwardly anxious but outwardly calm backseater.

"Hell yeah, Doc." Quintin was confident, but in-flight refueling over the desert took him to the edge. One wrong turn could bring instant disaster.

A few seemingly eternal minutes later, both thirsty Tomcats, now capped off with JP-5 fuel and full bellies, were vectoring north once more.

Just after sunset, while Quintin flew loose formation off his flight lead, he took a second or two to observe the geography below them from thirty-four thousand feet. It was slightly hazy, yet to his astonishment, the Euphrates River was in sight. He could see most of the smoke from the burning oil wells, with the plumes coalescing as the winds drifted the smoke over the Gulf. "Wow, Doc, take a look at the most famous river in the world. The cradle of civilization, baby." Quintin thought of Abraham from Ur, the Sumerians, and the Babylonians. Countless armies had crossed those sands in search of riches and conquest.

"Whatever," responded his RIO. "Focus on the mission in front of us. We're entering hostile territory. Need to be on the lookout for SAMs," he said, referring to surface-to-air missiles. The Iraqis had a Soviet version of the SA-2 capable of reaching and touching them even at that altitude.

"Yeah, yeah," Quintin radioed back on the intercom. He felt invincible and ready for anything.

Doc just shook his head and ignored his young pilot.

As they headed north, they flew just east of a city they recognized as Baghdad on their chart. Quintin couldn't help but stare at the ancient metropolis. He scanned the desert and hoped to see anything he could recognize as the ruins of Babylon. He thought of Ishtar Gate and imagined the hanging gardens. *Where are you?* He looked and looked but was unable to identify anything with certainty at that altitude. They continued loose formation off their lead, always wary of antiaircraft artillery and, mostly, the SAMs.

"Rage 205, this is Control. We have an unidentified bogey heading one zero zero degrees, climbing through two thousand feet at two hundred fifty knots. They are just east of you. Please identify. You are cleared to arm, but do not fire. Over."

"Roger, Control," responded Doc, who was the mission commander on the flight.

The two Tomcats banked hard right ninety degrees to put nose on the bogey. They accelerated to just below sonic speed as they chased the unknown aircraft heading away from them as it climbed.

"This isn't a helo. It's gotta be tac air," radioed Doc.

The rules of engagement at the time dictated that anything that was tactical—or tac air—was a threat and had to be neutralized. As both Tomcats acquired the target on their own radar, they screamed in speed as they closed in on their prey. The chase had begun fifteen miles apart, and now they were five miles in trail. Quintin's heart raced as he stayed in formation while trying to look ahead and see his potential target. To their frustration, the bogey was still climbing; however, it was still in a patch of clouds several thousand feet below and in front of them.

Oh no, thought Quintin. *This may be the real thing. Gonna get nasty.* He scanned behind both their aircraft to make sure there was no other unseen bogey coming up from the rear to ruin their day.

"Quintin, if the son of a bitch turns nose to us, I want you to blow him out of the sky!" ordered Doc.

"Yes, sir," he responded. Quintin originally selected Sparrow missiles, thinking those were better at their range, but as they got closer and closer, he switched to heat-seeking Sidewinders. He momentarily thought of gunning the poor bastard with their twenty-millimeter Vulcan cannon if the aircraft got any closer.

At two miles in trail of the bogey, it finally emerged from the cloud cover. "Com air. Com air," the flight lead said, broadcasting over the airwaves.

"Knock it off! Knock it off!" yelled the voice from the E-2 radar control aircraft.

Quintin and his flight lead pulled hard right and climbed away as they disengaged from the hunt. They had visually identified a commercial 727 flying from what was believed to be Saddam International Airport. "It's a fucking no-fly zone," radioed Doc. "Those crazy Iraqis were hoping we would shoot an airliner down and cause an international incident!"

Sons of bitches, thought Quintin. "Yeah, and we'd have to live with the fact that we'd vaporized more than a hundred civilians!"

After that encounter, Quintin's thoughts were no longer naive. The airwings task in support of Operation Desert Storm became more about survival and conscience to Quintin. He later told his father Ciso; "At the end of the day, to lay your head on a pillow without regrets is of great value." As their forty-five minutes on station ended, they made their way back to the tanker to cap off and headed for the ship.

After almost five hours in the cockpit, Quintin's bladder could hold no more. "Shouldn't have had those two cups of coffee before we left. What the hell was I thinking?"

"You're on hot mike, Quintin. Sure hope you have a piss bag," Doc said on the intercom.

Quintin selected autopilot, unfastened all his safety harnesses, grabbed the pee bag, and carefully unzipped his G suit and then flight suit. *What a pain in the ass just to pee*, thought Quintin. If they had to eject during Operation Golden Flow, he knew he was a goner.

After filling the bag, feeling relieved, he placed it in the glove box just to the right of his ejection seat and strapped everything on again.

It was well after midnight when they recovered back at the ship. The plane captain noticed the full pee bag and demanded Quintin handle his own baggage.

"Come on, Petty Officer Graves. What's a little urine between friends?" asked an amused Quintin.

"Sir, do you really want me to answer that?"

"No, not really." They both laughed.

Quintin grabbed his full container and flushed it at the nearest head. Exhausted, they debriefed the intel boys on their encounter. Quintin was planning to shower and head for the sack. "Rest up, boys; you're going back out tomorrow night," said the schedules officer.

With the throttles pulled back once outbound from Miramar NAS, the Tomcat responded faithfully. It was Doc's last flight in a fighter. He was headed to a desk job for his next duty rotation, and after that, he was thinking of retirement. That night's training mission was one versus two on intercepts in the military operations area (MOA) just offshore of San Diego, California. The aircraft headed out to open water and steadied on a southwesterly course. Their speed held steady at 250 knots, and they were level at an altitude of two thousand feet above sea level. Quintin released his oxygen mask as they headed out to their prearranged air stations. Over the water, a blanket of clouds obscured the sky above with the fading light of the afternoon slowly surrendering into darkness.

The ocean appeared calm and dark blue, almost black, under the low-lying clouds. *El Pacifico*, thought Quintin. He remembered having read about European explorer Balboa, who'd named the ocean due to its calm appearance while he was somewhere on the western coast of Panama in the sixteenth century.

As the Tomcat slowly ascended through the layer of clouds, it punched through the topside, revealing a seemingly unlimited sky above. The once overhead cloud cover now appeared like the ground of an alien world just below the jet. Glancing back, Quintin could see the groove in the cloud made by the aircraft. The sky above appeared a darker shade of blue and was bathed in gold by the waning light of the sun. It was a breathtaking sight. He wished he could share it with his wife, who was missing out on an amazing sunset. He watched the dazzling display of beauty. The sun's light beams raced across the sky, disturbed by an occasional wisp of high-altitude cirrus cloud. The mix of colors reminded him of a live tapestry created by an incredible artist. Quintin felt a sense of awe and gratitude at witnessing such perfection.

"Doc?"

"Yeah, bud?"

"Take a look at that sunset."

His RIO turned his attention from the large radar scope in front of him to the breathtaking sunset to the west. "Now, that's a sight," Doc said.

"Hey, Doc, do you believe in God?"

His RIO took his eyes off the sunset and looked forward at Quintin. "Well, I don't know too many atheists at three-quarters of a mile," he answered.

"Rampage 205, contact approach control on 208.3 on your return," instructed departure control.

"Roger. Out," responded Doc from the backseat. Then he added, "Okay, I've got two bogeys at our eleven o'clock, thirty miles," while staring at his radar.

"Roger," responded Quintin, and then he quickly glanced over at the left wingtip, remembering the mysterious bright light on his first carrier quals several years earlier. He often wondered about that unique one time incident. *It's not there*, he thought, and once again, he felt disappointed. Quintin had often hoped he would get another glimpse at that magnificent mystery.

Perhaps it was only there when I truly needed it but didn't expect it.

He then took one last look at the breathtaking sunset on the right side of his aircraft. Beautiful displays like that, he thought, were to be cherished and fully enjoyed in their short, passing perfection. He strapped his oxygen mask back on. "Let's go to work, Doc." He lit the afterburners, and they were pushed back in their seats as if two rockets had ignited to send them into Earth's orbit. The Tomcat started climbing to their tactical altitude to engage the bogeys in the MOA. "It's gonna be glorious, Doc."

"Damn straight, bud."

The F-14 B in full afterburner was the ultimate bird of prey. The navy's premier fighter and interceptor, although fun, was challenging to fly. It was one of the last, if not the last, US fighter with hydraulic flight controls and analog instrumentation. It was preparing to make way for the future, which included fly-by-wire and digital technologies, or electric jets, as they were called. Still, the men and women who flew and got to know that bird in an intimate way carved history into the halls of naval aviation. More endearing to Quintin than the aircraft were those who flew it and paved the way for future aviators. Some paid the ultimate price with their lives. Whether in training or in combat, F-14 pilots and their RIOs advanced US military aviation to new heights. "Anytime, anywhere" would always be the Tomcat's battle cry. Quintin would always remember that bird as a legendary masterpiece he'd had the privilege to pilot and would cherish the experience forever.

One year after Doc left the squadron, Quintin reentered civilian life. The F-14 had a short-lived advancement in a late model with more technological capabilities, but the navy ultimately decided to replace the F-14 permanently. On October 4, 2006, the Tomcat made its final flight before it was retired and stepped proudly into American aviation history.

CHAPTER 14

Awakening, December 2019

"How's the old man?"

Same question, different day. No change. Not one bit, thought Quintin. Ciso's appearance was depressing. Gone were the vitality, fervor, and zest for life he had been known for. The stubbornness and infectious energy he once had had were in the past. Atrophy, disconnection, noncommunication, and continued weight loss were ever increasing in his slow, murderous state of dementia. He was on a rapid path of aging, creeping toward the final end.

Even Margret, the perpetual optimist, had to acknowledge the inevitable.

"You know, Sis, dementia is a real bitch! It must really suck to get up and walk to the bathroom, and when you get there, you can't remember what you went in there for in the first place!" Quintin half smiled and forced a brief laugh.

Margret ignored him. Quintin could see the strain on his sister's face. She had carried the brunt of their father's care over the past two years, and it weighed on her. Ciso's slow deterioration was merciful in that he didn't seem to be in discomfort, yet the decay was like an exposed, ever-enlarging wound that would never heal. *God in heaven, let him rest. Death is welcomed over this slow, insidious decay*, Quintin prayed silently. Ciso's eyes had stayed mostly closed for the last few weeks, and he hardly uttered a word; at best, his communication was a grunt or mumble. When he did briefly open his eyes, they stared about the room as if staring at ghostly figures only he could see. Margret admitted it was creepy and sometimes said, "Maybe they are truly here, and we just can't see them."

"No way, no how, Sis. No such thing as ghosts, just malfunctioning neurons." Quintin silently hoped but was not truly convinced he actually believed what he said.

The last few months had taken a toll on Margret. Juggling work, home, and family while trying to be there for her father drained her tremendously. It was uncanny how her personality was similar to her father's. She had always been Daddy's little girl. Quintin often teased her for being just like him.

"Listen here, moron," she would say, using the stern rebuke she was well known for. Those who knew her steered clear of her explosive temper.

"She's the only woman I fear in this world," Quintin told others.

Members of the family often said, "Stay on her good side, because one day you'll go to sleep, and she'll make sure you never wake up!"

By the same token, she was always the first to empathize. She could be depended upon for just about anything, and she often gave all of herself for others. She truly had a servant's heart. However, in her anger, there was a point of no return. Even her husband trod carefully when she was angered.

With a heavy heart, Quintin got up from the side of his father's air-loss mattress, gave him a hug, and walked to the door. "Time to head back north and home."

"When do you think you'll be headed back this way?" asked his sister.

"Not sure," answered Quintin. *This may be the last time I see him alive. Though I felt like that last time too, so maybe he'll hang in there a little longer*, he thought.

Margret knew his thoughts. There was an uncomfortable silence in the room. As he stood at the door for several minutes, Quintin looked at the man he admired so much and had looked up to all his life, the man who had led his family to a distant country in search of freedom, independence, and self-reliance. Quintin and his sister were benefactors of their parents' sacrifice, hard work, and determination in overcoming barriers. Now there was just a shadow of the man he had known as his father. Little was recognizable.

Quintin, Margret, and their families knew the time was approaching. Ciso was on the edge; a common cold, an infection, or any small medical event would release him from the small grip he had on life. Quintin's thoughts momentarily turned to his mother, who had been gone for almost three years, and how he missed her. He turned to say goodbye to his sister. She then stepped out of the room to give him some time alone with his father. Quintin bowed his head in a heartfelt prayer. He then looked at his father, when, to his surprise, Quintin noticed Ciso's eyes were wide open and staring at him.

Ciso smiled and whispered, "Coqui," Quintin's childhood nickname.

At first, Quintin thought maybe his father was hallucinating again. As Quintin stepped forward and to his right, Ciso's eyes were locked onto his and followed his every movement. Quintin tried to take a breath. His heart beat faster at the realization that his father might have been aware of his presence. For the first time in almost two years, there appeared to be an acknowledgment of recognition.

Quintin was moved to tears. "Dad, *soy yo*" (Dad, it's me).

His father kept looking at him, still smiling, and then whispered his nickname once more. That was all he could get out. Moments later, Ciso rested his head back on the pillow, closed his eyes, and once again, as before, was expressionless. Quintin took his father's hand in his and held it.

Memories raced across Quintin's mind as he sat next to his father, still processing what had just transpired. "*Te quiero*," he told his father as his voice cracked under the weight of emotion. Quintin placed his head on his father's chest in a final emotional goodbye, thanking him for the father he had been and would always be in his heart. His last prayer was that his father, like his mother, would find peace with God.

Ciso remained in that locked-in state for another thirty days before his weak heart could go no further. Margret, her husband, and their daughter were there in his final moments. Ciso had lamented for many years not being there for his father's final moments in Cuba. Felix had died alone in a country hospital, hoping for one final glimpse of his family. Margret made sure her father didn't have the same fate. As the time grew near, she made sure to be at her father's side. Ciso was surrounded by family during his final hours. Perhaps he was aware of their presence. Quintin liked to think so. To Margret, it was important to be there.

At his passing, she called Quintin, who was nine hundred miles away. Upon hearing the news, Quintin took comfort in being surrounded by his own family.

CHAPTER 15

In the Smokies III

"Dad? Dad, it's me. Can you hear me? Please, Daddy, open your eyes. Joe is here too."

As Quintin recognized the voices of his children, their eyes slowly met. With a half smile, he reached out with his right hand to touch and feel their presence. "Yes," he muttered, now satisfied with the present reality. Like an old ship's ballast stones, his kids were keeping him upright and increasingly steady. Quintin scanned the room, hoping to grasp something familiar, but he could not. "What is this place? Where am I?"

As Quintin gathered his thoughts, the hospital surroundings were neat, orderly, and peacefully quiet, unlike the many standard hospital wings he had made many rounds on in his medical practice. "It sure would be nice if all hospital settings were to this standard," he whispered. With each passing minute, his awareness expanded, and clarity returned.

"We had you brought here from the main hospital. The doctors informed us you had a severe headache and high fever, and you became delirious."

"How long has it been? What was the fever from?"

"Only been a couple of days. They still don't know

193

where or how this began. But the good news is, the neurologist told us she doesn't think there will be any permanent symptoms."

The following day, Quintin felt stronger and was getting ready for discharge. He walked slowly to a chair by the window. Outside, he could see the sun's rays making their presence known across the parking lot several stories below. Several vehicles were transiting the lot, while a young couple made their way to their car with a baby in the woman's arms. At the edge of the asphalt, the tall pine trees lined up in formation like aviation officer candidates ready for marching drills.

His thoughts turned to Cari and their many years together. She had been gone for almost a month. Her loss was deep, and the emotional weight was bone-crushing. Cari's family had been at her side for the last few days before she finally succumbed to what physicians concluded was a large brain clot while fighting a severe viral respiratory infection. With Quintin's training and experience, the cause and mechanism were constantly cycling in his brain. He struggled to find answers, and over the days after her passing, he had been neglectful of his own needs. His obsession with finding the answers he sought, accompanied by unrelenting guilt, had cost him his own physical and emotional health. *Was it from her shunt placed so many years ago? Did she have a coagulation disorder activated by the infection?* Whatever it had been, the love of his life was no longer with him.

His intense grieving, followed by anger, was overtaking him. Deep sorrow slowly gave way as Quintin clung to precious hope. Loss made its arrival like a sudden blow, but hope was like the anticipation of a sunrise on a clear morning, with each passing minute bringing slow but steady renewal. The battle raged within him, and victories were small at first. "We will see each other again" slowly became his battle cry. *After all*, he concluded, *what is the totality of a human lifespan in the backdrop of eternity?*

Faith, he thought. Cari had had enough to fill a stadium. She'd had faith in things unseen, an assured hope, and she'd been confident it would come to be. *I sure could use more of that.*

While still looking at the vast forest beyond the parking lot, his thoughts and dreams of Cari were of enjoying their camping adventures. *If only it were so.*

"You've kept to yourself most of the night," said Cari.

"Sorry," said Quintin. "Lots of old memories, and I've been reflecting on Mom, Dad, and our family over the last thirty years. Where the heck have all the years gone? I'll be sixty soon. Can you believe that? Time is so merciless; it speeds up when you don't realize it, it waits for no one, and there are no replays. One minute you're enjoying hugs and kisses from little people who think you're the world, and then you blink, and the same little ones are grown and living their own lives, which don't often include you."

With a strain on his face, he stared at the fire, admiring its beauty. Each flame was unique and short-lived. "These flames remind me of humanity. It rises, shines in temporary glory, and then is gone. As I look back through our family's history, what do we have? Is it cause and effect?"

"What do you mean?" she asked.

"My parents came to these shores so many years ago in search of freedom and a better life. We are products of those decisions. This place, this time, our interwoven lives thrust together—is it all by chance, as if riding a strong current only to be washed ashore on some river's edge? Or is there a purpose to each and every one of us?"

Cari reached for her Nook and proceeded to read Ecclesiastes 12:13–14:

> Fear God and keep His commandments, for this is man's all, For God shall bring every work into judgement, including every secret thing, whether it be good or whether it be evil.

"I do not believe in a life by chance," she said. "I believe in purpose. God knows each of us intimately. He loves us and wants to have a personal relationship with each of us. Through that relationship, he will guide us and show us the way. We just have to believe and trust."

"This conversation is getting too deep. Let's talk about the weather," Quintin responded.

"What about regrets? Do you have any, and if so, would you change anything?" asked Cari.

"Frankly, I miss the simple things, like the company of those who raised and loved us and are no longer here. I miss the sounds of the little feet and sweet voices of our children, which are now only in memories. Though now, since they are in their teens, I think of murder. They both laughed as they pondered the challenges of raising young adults. Does that make me a bad father?" They laughed at the challenges of raising teenagers.

"Well, I'm gonna retire for the night. Join me soon?"

"Yes, I will be right there," responded Quintin as he stood and stretched, still looking at the flames of the campfire. He slowly turned toward the camper, closed his eyes, and breathed in deeply. The scent of burning hardwood reminded him of many camp experiences long ago with his parents. He listened in stillness, as if waiting for an approaching visitor. "What else is here?" he asked no one in particular. The silence was broken only by Cari in the camper as well as faint conversation and laughter from neighbors nearby.

When Cari came back out, he picked up the conversation where they had left off. "To those who are gone, I wish I could've said I'm sorry for any hurt I caused. I wish I would've chosen to love and not expect anything in return. So to answer your question, I would change some things if I could. But to live without regrets is to not be human. I don't want to sound cliché, but that's how I truly feel. Maybe you should not ask me a deep question before bed ever again."

They both smiled at the moment. Quintin and Cari had started an improbable relationship many years ago. After thirty years of marriage and countless challenges, they still were close, liked each other, and genuinely loved each other. There were several reasons, but at the center were the basic principles they'd embraced early in their marriage: divorce was never an option, they did not let the sun set on their anger, and they served each other. Cari had published a book reflecting on one of the most endearing subjects in her life: marriage and how to stay in it. In her publication, she'd illustrated the principles she lived by and the guidance and wisdom the Bible taught. It made him think about his parents' marriage and how different it had been from his. *My parents had different life experiences, and they had different goals and challenges. As with many couples, their closeness was fleeting and impersonal, at least from what I observed.*

"What about you, sweetie? Would you change anything? You recently told me things didn't quite turn out the way you imagined. You said, 'I could've been more lighthearted and not taken so many things so seriously.'"

"When I look back, I see that our generation had it much easier than our parents did. But their sacrifices were not in vain. Think about it: our worries were not their worries. Like so many immigrants, they left behind what they knew and those they loved. Why? For a better life for themselves and their children. Is that not the story of humanity?"

"I reckon so," answered Quintin. They both smiled at his southern response. "How do you feel about the future?" he asked her.

"The future? As long as we stay together and put God first in our lives, it will be okay," answered Cari. "By the way, did you hear anything about a virus coming out of China recently?" she asked.

"No," he responded. "Probably not a big deal. Besides, modern medicine is quite advanced and ready for those things."

"I love you."

"I love you too."

After thirty years of marriage, he was still crazy about her. That fourteen-year-old girl he'd met so many years ago at the pool was his best friend, and he couldn't imagine his life without her.

Cari went into the camper to prepare to retire for the evening, as she had done many times before on their camping adventures. Quintin followed her after a short while. While Cari was tidying up the kitchen, he gently approached her from behind, placed his hands on her waist, and gently kissed her neck and then her cheek. She slowly turned her head in his direction, ran her hands through his hair, and kissed him. He slowly reached over to close the blinds.

"Wait," she said. "Take the trash out, and then make sure to lock the door."

"*O cara*," he responded.

If I take the Wings of the morning, And
dwell in the uttermost parts of the sea,
Even there Your hand shall lead me, And
Your right hand shall hold me.

—Psalm 139:9–10 NKJV

Printed in the United States
by Baker & Taylor Publisher Services